The Forgotten Sky

Book One: The Veiled Truth Chronicles

A Novella

By JA Maren

Scripture quotations are from the King James Version (KJV) of the Bible, which is in the public domain, unless otherwise noted.
Select verses may be quoted or paraphrased from the following modern translations:
- *The Holy Bible, New International Version® (NIV)*. Copyright © 1973, 1978, 1984, 2011 by Biblica, Inc.™ Used by permission. All rights reserved worldwide.
- *The Holy Bible, English Standard Version® (ESV)*. Copyright © 2001 by Crossway, a publishing ministry of Good News Publishers. Used by permission. All rights reserved.

For more information, visit:
www.jamarenbooks.com

ISBN: 979-8-9985628-2-2

First edition, 2025

Dedication

This story is for the watchers.
For the ones who still believe the heavens declare.
For the ones who choose the narrow way,
even when it's lonely.

You are not alone.
And the sky was never silent.

Prologue

We've always been told the sky was empty.

That it stretched out into cold, silent infinity; a canvas of chance and chaos, sprinkled with stars too far away to touch, and too random to mean anything.

But the ancients didn't see it that way.

They called it a dome.

A firmament.

A boundary between what is seen and what is hidden. Not metaphor. Not myth. A veil.

Like all veils, it was meant to conceal something sacred.

Something dangerous.

For centuries, the knowledge was buried. Some say it was forgotten, while others say it was stolen. Scrubbed from textbooks, burned from scrolls, and mocked all in the name of progress. The sky was reduced to equations and theories.

We believed them. Because it was easier. Because it was safer. Because if the veil wasn't real...then neither was what waited behind it.

But there have always been witnesses. Whispers in the corners of crumbling seminaries. Scribbles throughout the margins of banned Bibles. Maps no telescope can explain. A thread running through Scripture and starlight, just waiting to be pulled.

And now, it has been.

My name is Claire Whitaker. I used to teach math until I found a notebook, and inside a question that changed everything. Because the sky is not what we were told and the truth... has always been above us.

Chapter One

It all started with a notebook.

Left on my desk like a forgotten assignment, no name, no class period, no cover. Just spiral-bound pages worn soft at the edges, bulging with clippings, taped inserts, scribbled notes, and more than a few verses underlined in red. I almost tossed it in the lost-and-found bin without a second thought.

But something made me open it.

The first page, upon cursory glance, just seemed like it contained a title. A blank page except for a single line of text. I almost skimmed past without a second thought, but for some reason I paused. The words carried a weight I couldn't explain. It was a message.

"THE FIRMAMENT IS REAL. THEY KNOW."

Nondescript, block letters. Black ink. Heavy pressure. Like whoever wrote it wanted the words to shout even if no one read them aloud.

I froze. Not because I believed them, at least not yet, but because of how it was written. It wasn't a theory. It wasn't even a question, no speculation or theory. It was a statement, stark and unapologetic. These words weren't trying to convince, or invite, they were a *warning*. But of what?

The more I stared at the page, the more something about the handwriting tugged at the edges of my memory. It felt oddly familiar, like I should recognize it. It took me until third period to place it.

Mason Daniels.

I first met Mason Daniels a year earlier. He was quiet then, almost painfully so—the kind of student who watched more than he spoke. But when he did speak—questions. Constant, relentless, thoughtful questions. About God. About physics. About the edges of things.

"Miss Whitaker," he once asked, "how do we know the Earth curves if we can't feel it?"
I'd laughed. "Because gravity." He hadn't laughed back. He was not being smug. He was being serious. I brushed it off. I'd brushed off a lot of things back then.

But something had changed over the past few months. He'd grown... restless. Like he'd found something he was not supposed to find. I'd seen the shift before in students who'd lost someone, or who'd stumbled into something too big for them to process. But Mason's shift did not come from grief.

Now I wondered if it came from truth.

He hadn't been to my class or school in over two weeks. There had been no explanation given. No withdrawal papers submitted from another school. Just an empty seat and a half-hearted comment from the school counselor: *"He's taking some time away for personal reasons."* The way she said it: flat, memorized, like she had rehearsed that line for days. There was no hesitation in her voice, no speculation about when he would return or how he was doing. And that told me all that I needed to know. She knew more than she was letting on and it wasn't just that she knew, but she was keeping a well-guarded secret.

After school, I took the notebook home. At first, I told myself it was just out of curiosity. That I'd glance through it once before tossing it back in my filing cabinet. But by midnight, I'd read the first five sections.

It wasn't rambling. It was research. Messy, yes. Disorganized, at times. But beneath the chaos, there was something structured. Deliberate. Layered like a code built out of pages and passages.

Verses from Genesis, Job, Psalms. Handwritten notes comparing translations. Cross-references to apocryphal texts. A recurring theme:

8

waters above the heavens, the vault of the sky, the dome stretched over the earth like a tent.

He wasn't quoting fringe websites.

He was quoting the Bible.

And then came the newspaper clippings. Yellowed photocopies of old articles, some dating back to the '50s, about Operation Highjump, Admiral Byrd, something called "Project Fishbowl." Each one marked in the margins: *They tried to break through.*

At first, I thought it was just a fringe fascination. The kind of thing lonely kids dive into online. But then I found the diagram.

A sketch of the earth: flat, enclosed by a dome. Layers labeled in tiny, neat handwriting. Waters above. Waters below. The stars were fixed, not floating. The sun and moon, moving, not still.

I held the drawing in my hands. Beneath the dome, Mason had scribbled something else, almost hidden in the margin: Genesis 1:6-8. And God said, let there be a firmament...

I'd grown up in church. Memorized that verse once in VBS. But I hadn't thought about it in years—not since Dad stopped going, not since I stopped believing prayer changed anything. It was evident Mason believed in something. Enough to write it down. Enough, maybe, to die for it.

And scrawled in red across the bottom:

"If this is true, what else have they lied about?"

I closed the notebook.

But I didn't, I couldn't put it away.

Instead, I sat at my kitchen table with a cup of cold coffee and my childhood Bible that I hadn't opened in years. It still smelled like old leather and highlighter. I flipped to Genesis 1:6. The words were there, plain as day.

"And God said, let there be a firmament in the midst of the waters, and let it divide the waters from the waters."

Not "atmosphere." Not "sky." Firmament.

The word was right there.

The footnotes didn't explain it.

And suddenly, I couldn't look away.

Chapter Two

I didn't sleep.

I tried, oh how I tried. Every time I closed my eyes; I saw that final page. "THE FIRMAMENT IS REAL. THEY KNOW." It wasn't just a phrase. It was a rift. A hairline crack in everything I thought was settled.

The next morning, my coffee tasted like paper, and the mirror showed shadows I hadn't yet earned. I told myself I was being ridiculous. Mason was grieving or processing. That the notebook was a coping mechanism. Even as I said it aloud in the bathroom, I didn't believe it.

I carried the notebook to school in my bag, tucked between lesson plans and a granola bar. I told myself I wouldn't read it during school hours. I was still a teacher. I had a job. I had other students who needed my attention.

During my planning period, I shut the door, pulled the blinds, and read.

This time, I noticed something new. A sticky note between pages 38 and 39. It hadn't been there before. Or maybe I just hadn't noticed. It read: *"If you found this, you were meant to. But be careful. They erase more than memories."*

Beneath it, a date was written March 3. Two weeks from now. And a location: Glenhaven Baptist Church — Back Lot — Midnight.

I stared at it. I hadn't heard Mason speak about church. Most kids didn't. Faith was either mocked or marketed these days, not lived. But this, this was something else. It wasn't religion. It was desperation.

I put the note back. Folded the page down.

In sixth period geometry, my hands trembled slightly as I wrote notes on the board. Triangle congruence felt like a foreign language. The students didn't notice; or if they did, they were too kind or too tired to say anything.

After school, I sat in my car with the engine off, holding the notebook in my lap. The parking lot emptied slowly. Teachers with bags of papers. Students laughing too loud. The mundane marched on.

Alabama spring sunsets could fool you—soft gold light turning to dark fast, like a switch. And yet, under it all, I felt a hum. A frequency not heard but sensed. Like the air had started remembering.

That night, I pulled out my Bible again and I flipped ahead. Psalms. Job. Amos.

"He stretches out the heavens like a curtain." "Can you bind the chains of the Pleiades?" "Seek Him that maketh the seven stars and Orion."

The stars weren't just lights. They were named. Ordered. Ruled.

I sat back on my couch and stared at the ceiling. As if it were hiding something. Because maybe, just maybe, it was. Maybe there was more out there than we'd ever been taught.

I didn't sleep that night either. I lay awake in bed, staring at the ceiling, hearing faint cracks in the walls like the house itself was holding its breath. The notebook was on the table beside my bed. And sometime around 2 a.m., I heard it.

A whisper. Not in the air. In me.

It said: "The heavens declare the glory of God—but the world has forgotten how to listen."

Chapter Three

Ezra Holt wasn't the kind of teacher who drew attention. He taught history the old-fashioned way, through lectures, timelines, yellowed maps, and primary sources. No flair. No gimmicks. But the students listened. They said he made the past feel haunted, like something you couldn't shake off.

I never paid much attention to him outside of faculty meetings. We taught in different wings of the school. We nodded in the hall, exchanged staff lounge pleasantries. That was all, until the notebook.

It was two days after I found the notebook when I caught him watching me. It was subtle, just a glance across the hall as I locked my classroom door. But something about the look made me pause. Not suspicious or creepy. More like... knowing. Like he recognized what I was carrying before I did.

I'd started staying late after school. Not because of grading or meetings, but because the silence helped me think. When the last student left and the fluorescent lights flickered to life in the empty hallways, the building changed. It breathed differently. Held its secrets closer. Some days I wondered if it was trying to keep me out—or invite me in.

That evening, as I passed the history wing on my way to the main office, he stepped into the hallway and said my name.

"Claire."

I stopped.

He looked around, then motioned me into his classroom. The lights were low. The windows cracked. A projector sat idle on his desk, paused on a slide about the Council of Nicaea.

"What do you know about the firmament?" he asked.

I blinked. "Excuse me?"

Ezra gestured toward a book on his desk. He had an old leather-bound copy of the Geneva Bible. It was open to Genesis 1.

"I saw you reading during lunch," he said. "Saw the notebook too. You found his, didn't you?"

He didn't have to say Mason's name. I nodded slowly.

He leaned back against the edge of the desk. "You should know you're not the first to ask questions. Mason wasn't either."

I felt suddenly exposed, like the walls had ears.

"You knew him?" I asked.

Ezra nodded. "Mason asked the questions no one else would. He came to me with passages and verses about the firmament, the sun and moon inside it, the waters above. He wasn't just theorizing. He was tracing a pattern. And he found it."

"What kind of pattern?"

Ezra lifted a folder from his desk and opened it. Inside were photocopies of pages from ancient commentaries, 19th-century sermons, and old encyclopedias. Each one referencing a literal heaven, a barrier between waters, and the earth as fixed and enclosed.

"This isn't fringe," Ezra said. "It was orthodoxy for centuries and wasn't until the 1900s that things started changing. Quietly. Strategically. Even seminaries stopped teaching it."

"Why?"

He paused. "Because the sky tells the truth. And truth has always been dangerous to those who build power on lies."

I sat down without meaning to. The room felt heavier now.

Ezra pulled out a small, laminated card from his wallet. It was a photograph of Wernher von Braun's tombstone with the inscription: *Psalm 19:1.* "The heavens declare the glory of God," Ezra quoted. "But most people don't ask what heavens really means."

We sat in silence for a long time. The classroom buzzed with the faint hum of the old heater.

"Mason was on to something," Ezra finally said. "But he wasn't reckless. He documented everything. If someone took him—if he's missing—it's because he saw something they didn't want seen."

I felt my pulse in my throat. "You believe that?" I asked.

Ezra looked at me, steady. "I've seen what happens to people who ask the wrong questions. But I've also seen what happens to those who stay silent. You must decide which weight you'd rather carry."

He told me about others: a professor who vanished before publishing a controversial paper, a seminary student whose thesis on ancient cosmology was deleted from every database, a linguist who connected ancient scripts to symbols found in satellite data. Each of them had one thing in common: they began asking questions that made the wrong people uncomfortable.

I left the room with the Geneva Bible tucked under my arm.

And I didn't look back.

Chapter Four

The next few days were a blur of half-taught Geometry lessons and late-night reading. I kept Mason's notebook under my pillow, like it might whisper to me while I slept. The Geneva Bible stayed on my desk at home, open to Genesis 1, the words *firmament* and *waters above* now etched into my mind like scars.

At school, I taught congruent triangles and parallel lines, but my mind was tracing other angles, ancient ones, heavenly ones. Every empty hallway felt like a secret waiting to surface. Every flicker of fluorescent light overhead seemed to pulse in time with a truth buried too long.

Ezra kept his distance. We didn't talk in public. But once, he passed me a folded article in the staff lounge when no one was watching. It was a scan of an 1867 sermon attributed to Charles Spurgeon: *"When God made the heavens, He placed them above the firmament and separated the waters beneath. That sacred division yet stands, though man in his pride may deny it."*

I stared at the words the entire walk back to my classroom.

At home, I spread Mason's notebook across my kitchen table like it was scripture. He'd clipped a page labeled "Operation Fishbowl" with a rusted paperclip. At the top was a sketch of a missile, and beneath it, a block of text in red ink: 1958. High-altitude nuclear tests. Claimed: atmospheric research. Reality: they hit something. I read the word hit three times before I turned the page.

Taped beside his notes was a grainy photograph—a blast suspended mid-air in a way that defied gravity. It wasn't a mushroom cloud. It looked like light smashing against something unseen. Mason had written beneath it: They weren't studying. They were testing the ceiling.

I opened my laptop. Government sites told the same polished story: high-altitude tests over Johnston Atoll, designed to study the magnetosphere. Clinical language. Scientific euphemisms. All of it carefully wrapped in "nothing to see here." But buried on an archived forum, I found a post from a deleted user named EchoWitness: "I worked on the fringe of Starfish Prime. One of the techs said the blast did not expand outward. It rebounded. Like it hit a dome." The post was dated 2006. The account was gone. Of course it was.

I called my dad that night. We hadn't spoken in months. He used to work as a systems engineer—communications, mostly. Some contracts with aerospace. I never asked questions. Until now.

"Did you ever hear about Operation Fishbowl?" I asked.

There was a long pause. "Where'd you hear that?"

"Old research."

Another pause. Then: "I knew a guy once. Said they were trying to measure the edge of something. He never called it a dome, but he said... there were boundaries. And they didn't like that we found them."

"They?"

"People who give orders. People who think the truth should come in pieces, not whole."
He didn't say more. I didn't ask him to.

That night, I couldn't sleep. I flipped through Mason's notebook again. Tucked between two pages was a yellowed excerpt from the Book of Enoch: "And the stars of heaven transgressed their order and were bound in valleys of the earth until the day of judgment." Under it, Mason had written in red: It's not about flat or round. It's about sealed and silenced. I stared until the letters blurred.

The next day, during my planning period, I went to the library.

Our school librarian, Mrs. Hayward, had been there for thirty years. She wore earth-toned sweaters and moved like a ghost among the shelves. I asked if we still had the older science encyclopedias, anything published before 1950.

She raised an eyebrow but said nothing. She led me to a back cabinet and unlocked it with a key from around her neck. "Why these?" she asked.

"Just curious," I replied.

She hesitated, then said quietly, "Be careful what you get curious about, Claire. They've pulled better teachers for less."

I didn't ask what she meant.

Inside the cabinet, I found a set of encyclopedias from 1923. Volume E was the one I needed.

I flipped to the entry for *Earth*.

Earth, according to the Scriptures and ancient cosmologies, is a fixed plane surrounded by the firmament—a solid barrier which divides the heavens from the terrestrial realm. The stars are set in this firmament, and the sun and moon move within it.

My breath caught. It wasn't a fringe idea. It was in the books they no longer let students read.

Back in my classroom, I copied the entry by hand into Mason's notebook. And that night, I found something else.

Pressed between two pages near the back, there was a photograph— grainy, probably a newspaper scan. A man stood beside a chalkboard covered in star patterns and concentric rings labeled in Hebrew.

On the back, scribbled in red pen: "*Gideon. Last one to teach it openly.*"

Beneath it, an address in tiny print.

I knew what I had to do.

But first, I had to see if Gideon was still alive.

And if he remembered the sky we were never supposed to forget.

Chapter Five

Ezra drove. We didn't say much on the way, just shared a look when we passed the county line. He knew this road too. Mason had brought him once to meet Gideon.

Gideon lived two towns over in a cottage that looked like it belonged to another century. The address led us down a gravel road, past a wooden sign with a faded verse from Isaiah: *"Lift up your eyes on high and behold who hath created these things."* The place had the quiet dignity of someone who had stopped caring what the world thought a long time ago.

I knocked once. Then again. The door creaked open.

"Claire Whitaker?" he asked before I could speak. He was older than I expected, maybe mid-seventies, but sharp-eyed, with ink-stained fingers and the kind of voice that sounded like it had weathered decades of sermons no one wanted to hear.

"I knew your grandfather," he said, ushering us in. "He was one of the last to teach the firmament as literal truth."

I froze. "My grandfather?"

Gideon nodded. "A math teacher too, wasn't he? He never separated numbers from heaven. Knew the sky moved in patterns; patterns no spinning globe could explain."

Inside, his walls were lined with books, old ones. No dust jackets. No barcodes. Many in Greek and Hebrew. There were rolled maps in the corners, diagrams pinned to corkboards, and a telescope, not pointed towards the sky, but sideways, toward a mirror.

"I've been watching the watchers," Gideon said. "And I've been waiting." He pulled a notebook from a drawer and flipped to a page. "This is what Mason found."

It was a chart. Genesis references lined up against Babylonian, Egyptian, and Hebrew cosmologies. In all of them, the earth was fixed. The heavens above. The waters divided. A firmament in between.

"They all said the same thing," Gideon said. "Until science decided to serve something else."

I studied the chart. So did Ezra, who had joined me inside and now stood silently by the door.

"But why hide it?" I asked. "Why erase what Scripture says so plainly?"

Gideon's face hardened. "Because if there's a firmament, then someone had to put it there. If the stars are fixed, then someone fixed them. And if the earth doesn't move, then man isn't the measure of all things. God is."

Ezra spoke quietly. "That's a truth the modern world can't tolerate."

Gideon nodded. "So, they replaced it. Not with better truth, but with control. Indoctrination they dressed up as education."

He pulled out a textbook from 1899 and held it next to one from 2023. "Compare them. One begins with God's design. The other with human theory."

We sat for hours: talking, reading, listening. Gideon showed us star trails that bent only when processed through modern software. He played a recording of a scholar who tried to submit a paper on geocentric models to a theology journal and was blacklisted.

Before we left, Gideon handed me a folded page. "This," he said, "is what got your grandfather fired." It was a transcript of a sermon: "The sky does not lie. It declares. It remembers. And it waits. The only question is whether we are still willing to look up."

I felt something stir in me. Not rebellion. Not fear.

Conviction.

Outside, the stars blinked into place, like old friends returning.

Ezra looked up, hands in his coat pockets. "I think I believe it now," he said.

I did too.

And I knew—whatever came next—I wouldn't be able to unsee it. Not ever again.

Chapter Six

It started with the chalk, slipping from my fingers halfway through first period. Then again. And again. By the fourth drop, I gave up and switched to dry-erase. But even that felt wrong. The board swam, the lines blurred. Geometry had once grounded me, a language of proof and reason. Now it felt like I was trying to solve an equation written in smoke.

I told myself it was the coffee. Or the sleepless nights. Or the residual stress of the visit with Gideon. But deep down, I knew better. The shaking wasn't physical. It was spiritual. A tremor running through the framework of things I thought I understood.

By second period, I had to grip the whiteboard to keep steady. I started sketching triangle congruence, only for the marker to hesitate mid-stroke—just slightly—like the surface had shifted beneath my hand. A shimmer. A ripple. Gone as fast as it came.

I turned. The room was silent. Lila sat in the front row, watching me carefully. Her hand was half-raised, hesitant. "Miss Whitaker? Are you okay?"

I nodded stiffly. "Just tired." She didn't believe me. I didn't believe me. The bell rang. As the students filtered out, I caught movement near the windows. A figure.

Daniel Morgan.

He wasn't in this class. Hadn't been all semester. But there he was, sitting at a desk near the back: his shoulders tense, eyes glazed like he was looking through the walls.

"Daniel?" I called.

He didn't respond.

I moved toward him, heart thudding.

And then—he was gone.

Not walked out. Not disappeared. Just... no longer there. The desk empty. No bag. No trace.

I had to get myself together, everything at school felt too small. The hallways, the lesson plans, the questions on the board. I walked through them like a ghost, like someone caught between the world that is and the one that had been hidden just behind it.

Ezra and I kept our conversations brief and coded. He slipped me a copy of a 19th-century theological tract under a worksheet on quadratic equations. I handed him a newspaper clipping from the 1940s tucked inside a lesson on statistical reasoning. We were teachers. That gave us cover.

But it also gave us reach.

It was during one of my library visits that I found the book—wedged behind a dusty thesaurus, spine cracked, and gold-leaf title almost worn away: *Foundations of Ancient Cosmology.* I opened it and nearly dropped it.

Inside were diagrams that mirrored everything Mason had drawn. An enclosed earth. Waters above. The luminaries on tracks. It cited Scripture with reverence and clarity—and not just Genesis. Psalms. Job. Isaiah. Even Revelation. The firmament wasn't metaphorical. It was structural. Purposeful. I looked at the library catalog sticker. It hadn't been checked out in over 20 years.

That night, I scanned every page into a private folder. By midnight, I had read through the book twice.

The next day, Ezra asked me to meet after school. We sat in his classroom, blinds drawn. He was holding a copy of *Science and Scripture*, dated 1910. "They used to teach this in seminary," he said.

I nodded. "Until they didn't."

We didn't say anything for a while. Just sat in silence, reflecting.

Finally, Ezra leaned forward. "I've been thinking. If we want to trace this, really trace it, we need to follow the pattern of erasure. We have to find out when they stopped printing this, when schools changed curriculum, when churches shifted theology. There's a timeline here. A method."

I added, "Someone, somewhere had to sign off on it."

We began mapping it out, decade by decade. What was removed. What was added. Who benefited. By the time the bell rang the next morning, we had a wall full of post it notes, strings, and quotes.

Mason hadn't been chasing a theory.

He had been uncovering a crime.

Chapter Seven

I hadn't stepped foot inside a church in nearly six years. Not since Mom's funeral. Not since my father's voice cracked while reading Psalm 23 and I realized he was saying the words, not believing them. Church had stopped being sacred to me that day. It became a stage: wooden floors, stained glass, and rehearsed smiles.

However that following weekend, I went to visit my mother's grave for the first time in months. She had believed in God with a quiet, unwavering faith, the kind that didn't ask for signs or question the curriculum. I wondered now what she would say if she knew what I was seeing, what I was uncovering. Would she have thought I was straying, losing my mind, or would she have reminded me that God never asked us to stop seeking?

The wind stirred the edges of the notebook in my hand. I knelt, brushed the leaves from her stone, and whispered, "They lied to us, Mom. About more than science. About everything. Everything I've ever been taught is a lie."

I felt no answer. But I also felt no fear.

Back at my apartment, I found an envelope taped to the inside of my screen door. No name. No return address. Just a worn envelope sealed with red wax.

Inside: a photograph. Grainy. Old. A man standing before a wooden lectern in what looked like a chapel. Behind him, a chalkboard with concentric rings—earth, firmament, waters above. The man was labeled in pen: "Gideon. 1974."

With it was a short note: "They silenced him before. They'll try again."

There was one more item inside. A flash drive.

I hesitated only a moment before plugging it in. On it: a single folder titled PROJECT: VEIL. Inside, videos, transcripts, and scans of internal memos. Most were dated between 1999 and 2006. All pointed to one thing: They weren't just hiding the firmament.

They were building something to replace it.

And the name of the initiative chilled me: Operation Blue Veil.

Chapter Eight

Ezra and I spent the next three days buried in files.

Most of the documents from the flash drive had been scrubbed of context—no letterheads, no names. But the language was clear. They spoke of "frequency shielding," "subliminal geospatial interference," and "constructive inhibition of ancient consciousness."

"What does that even mean?" I asked, pointing to one memo.

Ezra frowned. "It means they're using sound. Vibration. Frequency. Not to enlighten, but to suppress. To maintain a barrier and maintain a controlled environment."

Project Blue Veil wasn't just replacing the sky metaphorically. It was masking something.

One folder included diagrams of installations; massive towers arranged in geometric patterns. Some I recognized. Some I didn't. But their locations formed a net. A net over the world.

The final file was a short video. Static. Then a voice, heavily distorted: "The veil must remain. The threshold cannot be crossed. Consciousness must stay confined until protocol completion."

The audio cracked, a ripple of interference.

"I started with Genesis. Because that's where the veil is thinnest. People think it's poetry. But it's blueprint. The firmament isn't a metaphor. It's a structure. And they knew. The early church fathers. The ancient rabbis. Even NASA knows, they're not hiding science. They're hiding the shape of obedience."

Another pause.

"I did not believe it at first either. But the deeper I went, the more I discovered; maps with missing continents, stars that don't behave like they should, men in gray suits who show up before you say anything out loud."

We stared at the screen long after it faded, not speaking.

We just sat still, the silence ringing louder than the recording ever had. Somewhere along the way, I'd convinced myself that what Mason had found was something he was not ready for. Now I realized it was something we all weren't meant to find. And someone had been keeping it that way for a very long time.

Finally, Ezra leaned back, pale. "They're afraid of something waking up."

"Or someone," I whispered.

That night, I stared at the ceiling for a long time, no longer wondered what the stars might say. I wondered how long we had been deaf to them.

Later that night, I pulled out the notebook again. This time, something was taped to the back cover I'd never noticed before.

A small envelope. Inside it was a photograph. A polaroid, slightly faded, showing a mural—an old church wall, half-crumbling. Painted on it: a dome covering the earth, with fire beneath and stars above.

The caption at the bottom read: Calvary Hollow, 1974. Mural removed after complaints.
On the back, in Mason's handwriting: "Not all history is erased. Some of it is buried."

Chapter Nine

The photo led us to a small chapel just outside Franklin County. The building had been boarded up for decades, but Ezra found the land deed registered under a Gideon L. Graves.

We arrived just before dusk. The stained glass was shattered, but the bones of the building held. Inside, dust motes danced in the last light of day.

"Look there," Ezra said, pointing to the lectern.

It was the one from the photograph of Gideon. The chalkboard, though now cracked, still bore the faint outline of the rings.

Tucked inside the pulpit, we found a journal. Leather-bound. Initialed G.G.

Gideon's notes. They were half sermon, half warning. Pages and pages of scriptural cross-references about the heavens, the stars as signs, and the firmament as not just a division—but a witness. One entry read: "They called me mad when I refused the new curriculum. But I would not teach lies. The heavens declare His glory. I will not declare man's replacements."

Another: "The towers went up the same year they removed Genesis 1:6 from the student catechism."

I closed the journal gently. Ezra's voice was quiet. "We're not just following clues anymore."

"No," I said. "We're standing where someone was silenced. And I think they knew we'd find this."

From outside came the sound of a car door. Ezra and I locked eyes. And the chapel grew still.

The sound of the car door froze us both. Ezra reached for the flashlight on the pew, flicking it off. We crouched behind the lectern, hearts pounding. The chapel was so still we could hear the wind outside shift through the broken panes.

Footsteps crunched on gravel. Slow. Deliberate.

I glanced at Ezra. He nodded once, silently. If we had to run, we'd go through the back—where the floor was weaker, but open.

The footsteps stopped.

Silence. Then retreating. The sound of a car engine. A turn. Gravel scattering beneath tires.

We waited another full minute before moving. "Could've been anyone," I whispered.

"Or someone who knows what this place is," Ezra said.

We left soon after. But we came back early the next morning. We weren't sure why; maybe because the silence from the night before still pressed on us like a held breath. Or maybe because some places don't give up their secrets in a single visit.

This time, we brought tools: gloves, flashlights, notebooks. Ezra brought his grandfather's Bible, the one he said had led him into teaching history instead of preaching. "Scripture's deeper than they let on," he told me once. "And history is what they rewrite when they want you to forget."

We pried open a back room that had been nailed shut. Inside was a storage area full of decaying hymnals and broken pew legs. But one section of the back wall looked newer. Cleaner.

I ran my hand along the brick and stopped at a hollow sound. "Here," I said.

We took turns chipping at the mortar. After ten minutes, a section gave way—and behind it, wrapped in cloth, was a single book, hand-bound. Thick. The cover read: *The Cosmological Archives of G. L. Graves.*

We didn't speak. We just carried it to the front pew and sat down.

The pages inside were astounding. They didn't contain theory, they held proof. Star charts that matched pre-NASA sky maps. Hebrew word studies showing the firmament (*raqia*) as a solid dome. Historical footnotes on early explorers who reached the edge—not the poles, but something they were told not to speak of.

There were transcriptions of interviews with old pastors, rabbis, and missionaries who had seen anomalies—light that bent the wrong way, water that reflected stars too clearly, seismic recordings that stopped flat at certain frequencies.

Graves had written in the margins of nearly every page.

"We've traded God's design for man's delusion."

"The curriculum silences the cosmos."

"The veil is not just above—it's within."

At the very back, a folded sheet of tracing paper bore a map—hand-drawn and incomplete—but it showed concentric circles radiating from a central point. Not continents. Not countries.

Domains.

Ezra turned to me. "This changes everything."

I nodded. "We need to find the rest."

Chapter Ten

We scanned the pages and uploaded everything to an encrypted drive. Then we began our search.

The phrase *Cosmological Archives* turned up nothing online—but buried in the footnotes of an obscure 1871 seminary paper, we found mention of a traveling scholar who spoke in "hidden gatherings" across the South. Gideon Graves.

Each location listed lined up with places where school boards had radically shifted their curriculum in the mid-20th century.

"They didn't only erase," Ezra said. "They replaced and then they salted the ground."

We started driving. County to county. Library to library. Old churches, historical societies, abandoned schools. Sometimes we found nothing. Other times—treasures: fragments of Gideon's maps, microfilm reels of banned textbooks, sermon transcriptions with red stamps across the pages: *Not Doctrinally Aligned.*

In one town, a retired pastor gave us a box from his attic. "Didn't think anyone still cared," he said. Inside were cassette tapes labeled "Gideon Lectures." We played one in the car.

"The veil isn't just deception—it's engineering. A construct of control. And only when men fear God again will the sky open."

Ezra gripped the wheel tighter. "He's not just describing physics. He's describing repentance."

The next location, a school library, wasn't large, but it held more than just books. It held time. Dust. Echoes. When I pushed open the double doors after hours, the fluorescent lights buzzed overhead like hesitant witnesses. Ezra followed silently behind me; his satchel slung over his shoulder.

We weren't here for textbooks. We were here for the archives: old annuals, microfiche, forgotten maps tucked in crumbling folders. Anything that might tell us what this town had once known. Anything that hadn't yet been scrubbed or digitized out of memory.

"Why here?" I asked.

"Because this school was built in the forties," Ezra said. "Back when people still questioned what they saw in the sky. Before the narrative hardened. Before the textbooks were all rewritten."

We dug through drawer after drawer, and slowly, the truth began to flicker to life in fragments. One file stood out: a torn newspaper clipping from 1957—LOCAL STUDENT EXPELLED FOR UNORTHODOX SCIENCE FAIR PROJECT. The photo showed a boy in a suit beside a poster board shaped like a dome.

Ezra leaned closer. "His name was Jasper Tilley. Mason mentioned him in a margin note. Said his grandfather had hand-drawn star maps using a circular horizon."

I studied the photo. The hand-labeled diagram. The look of conviction on Jasper's face. "Ezra... this map matches the one from Genesis to Revelation. The four corners. The waters above. A throne above the firmament."

We photocopied it. As we dug deeper, we found more. More drawings, more correspondences, more anonymous tracts tucked inside hymnals. Then, in a locked drawer behind the librarian's desk, an envelope labeled DO NOT CIRCULATE. Inside: three pages of hand-sketched diagrams, a biblical timeline from Eden to the present, and a warning scrawled at the bottom.

If you find this, remember: the sky lies. But the Word never does.

Our hands trembled. It wasn't just about exposing a lie. It was about calling the world to remember the truth.

By the end of that week, we had more than we started with but far less than we needed. Some pages were missing. And, come to find out, we weren't the only ones looking.

We knew because one night, we came back to my apartment and the drive was gone.

The lock on the door wasn't broken. The windows were intact.

But the truth had been stolen and the silence that followed was louder than ever before.

Chapter Eleven

We didn't call the police. There was no sign of forced entry, and we both knew what a report would do. Most likely it would be ignored, or it would bring the wrong kind of attention. Either way we didn't want to call attention to what we were doing.

Ezra changed the locks. I called an old friend who knew about signal jammers, and she recommended a Faraday pouch for anything electronic. We also started taking notes by hand.

Ezra and I went to the school on Monday as if nothing had changed. Pretending normal still existed. While everything had, in fact, changed so completely that it was almost unrecognizable. We both felt it. The way our classrooms hummed under the fluorescent lights, the way emails arrived at just the wrong time, the way conversations in the teacher's lounge dropped into silence when we walked in.

Later that day, I was called into Principal Carson's office. It was after fourth period. The fluorescent lights above buzzed faintly, and his office smelled like old coffee and carpet cleaner. I sat down without being asked.

"We've had some... comments," he said, flipping through a manila folder with more flair than necessity.

I raised an eyebrow. "Comments?"

"Anonymous, of course. But they're worth discussing." He leaned back, lacing his fingers. "It's about your content."

"I've been teaching geometry. Proofs. Angles. Real edge-of-the-seat stuff."

He did not smile. "That's not the concern. Someone mentioned you've been introducing... off-topic material. Concepts outside the approved state curriculum."

I exhaled slowly. "You mean when students ask questions?"

"I mean what you choose to say in response."

I stared at him. "Are we not allowed to encourage critical thinking anymore?"

He gave the practiced principal smile—thin, polite, and completely unamused. "Just keep it aligned with the textbook. We don't want parents calling the board." He stood up to end the meeting but added casually, "Also, your classroom computer flagged some unusual web activity. You might want to check your browser settings."

I blinked. "I haven't used that computer for anything but slides and attendance."

"I'm sure it's nothing." He smiled again. "Just a heads-up."

When I left the office, I felt the eyes before I saw them. Someone peering through the front office window, the secretary maybe, or someone who moved away before I could get a good look. But the feeling stayed with me the rest of the day. I was being watched. Not by students. Not even by staff. By something behind the scenes.

A note appeared in Ezra's mailbox. No envelope. Just a folded sheet of paper.

"He spoke at Larkspur Chapel. 1983. Check the ledger."

We drove out that night. The chapel was abandoned, but the records hadn't been. A small museum across the street kept a dusty archive. Inside a leather guestbook from the fall of '83, Gideon's name was there along with the words "Ezekiel's Horizon."

Ezra muttered, "That's not a sermon title."

We found a pamphlet tucked in the back. It described a private gathering hosted by a group called The Horizon Fellowship. Attendees were by invitation only. The stated purpose: *to remember the firmament.*

We tracked that name, The Horizon Fellowship, to three other mentions. All were in rural towns, all tied to missing persons or unexplained church fires.

It wasn't just a whisper network of believers. It had once been an underground fellowship, a loose coalition of pastors, scholars, and laymen exchanging letters, coded pamphlets, and sermons that dared challenge the modern cosmological narrative. They met in back rooms, barns, and basements. Anywhere the questions could be asked without consequence.

It had been dismantled quietly, systematically. Not with headlines or raids, but with rumors, transfers, revoked credentials, and suspicious fires. They weren't just hiding; they were being erased.

That night, Ezra stayed at my apartment. We watched the sky, the stars strangely still. I asked him what he thought it all meant.

He didn't answer right away. Then he said, "The veil is more than a cover-up. It's a counterfeit.

And what's coming... they're going to sell it as salvation."

Chapter Twelve

We needed help. Not just books and voices from the past, but someone alive who could connect the threads.

I remembered Mason had once mentioned a professor, Dr. Helen Reyes, who'd been blacklisted from a major university after questioning the lunar missions. She lived off-grid in Tennessee now, according to a blog post archived in one of Mason's browser caches.

We made the drive in a single day. Dr. Reyes lived in a cabin surrounded by antennas, goats, and a massive satellite dish pointed at nothing. Encircled by overgrown rose bushes and the faint scent of cedar. She greeted us with pruning shears and suspicion.

"You here to laugh or to listen?"

"Listen," Ezra said. "And maybe ask about the maps."

She let us in. Her living room was a sanctuary of old books, hand-drawn maps, and celestial charts tacked to the walls. A wood stove crackled in the corner.

We sat on the couch as she served us black tea and unlocked a storage trunk filled with reel-to-reel tapes. "They let me go because I asked one question too many," she said. Like "Why do satellites only exist in CGI? I had started seeing the patterns thirty years ago," she said. "The alignments. The anomalies. Things that didn't match the globe projections. They tried to bury it. Redefine it."

She showed us a chart—circular, with concentric rings and coordinates mapped over scripture verses. Above it, Psalm 104:5 was scribbled in ink: *Who laid the foundations of the earth, that it should not be removed forever.*

Then came the stories of magnetic anomalies suppressed in government documents, towers built on ancient sites, and energy patterns linked not to latitude but to liturgy. The land, she believed, held memory. And memory, when threatened, fights back.

Next, she showed us footage from a 1989 interview with a young scholar who'd connected early weather balloon anomalies to the Van Allen radiation belt and then back to the idea of a barrier. "The problem," she said, "is that the evidence isn't missing. It's mislabeled."

She leaned in close, her voice almost a whisper. "There was a broadcast once. A documentary scheduled to air in 1996. It linked ancient cosmology with new geophysical data. It was pulled an hour before airtime. Every copy destroyed... except this."

Before we left, Dr Reyes handed us a VHS tape. Scribbled in red marker: *THE FORGOTTEN SKY*.

We watched it that night. And it was everything. Truth layered in allegory. Footage layered with Scripture. Testimonies from whistleblowers who had vanished. A warning about a coming deception so global, so spiritual, that even the elect might be deceived.

Ezra whispered, "This was the wake-up call before the power cut."

We stayed up until dawn. And for the first time, I realized: This wasn't about proving a theory. It was about preparing for a storm.

The tape had a name scrawled on the spine in faded pen: "E. Hargrave." It meant nothing to us. But when Ezra ran it through an academic database, the name came up only once: an astronomy professor who published a single paper in 1971, then vanished from all records.

The paper was called *Celestial Mechanics in Ancient Hebrew Thought*.

We found a photocopy in the local university's microfilm archive. In it, Hargrave argued that early biblical cosmology wasn't primitive, it was precise. The stars weren't just lights; they were signs, set in order by a designer who had encoded time, seasons, and prophecy into the very dome above us.

He cited Psalm 19: "The heavens declare the glory of God; the skies proclaim the work of his hands... Day after day they pour forth speech." Not metaphor, he insisted. Signal.

Ezra looked at me. "He believed the stars were talking."

On the last page of the paper, Hargrave mentioned an unpublished manuscript: *The Dome as Clock*. It was never cataloged. But a handwritten note listed a post office box in North Carolina.

It was a long shot, but we drove there. The box was still active.

The clerk wouldn't give us any info, but when I slipped her, a note explaining we were Hargrave's former students working on a memorial exhibit, her expression softened. There was a flicker of recognition, or maybe just sympathy. She glanced around, then nodded and handed me a plain envelope without another word.

Inside: a folded map of the constellations. Overlaid symbols. Hebrew letters. A code.

Ezra's voice shook. "This isn't just a star chart. It's a countdown."

Chapter Thirteen

We didn't sleep that night. We cross-referenced everything starting with Genesis, Psalms, Ezekiel, Revelation. From the firmament to the fountains of the deep, from the rainbow to the judgment fire. The structure was all there. Not metaphor. Blueprint.

Ezra opened Mason's journal again. One line, circled in red, stood out: *They'll use heaven to hide hell.*

A knock at the door froze us.

We stared at each other in silence. Waiting. Listening. Nothing, no footsteps, no retreating shadows. Just a manila envelope, slid under the door.

Inside: a satellite image of the Arctic. But something was wrong. A shimmer, a warping at the pole. Not ice. Not clouds.

A tear in the curtain.

Typed across the bottom: *You're not the first to see it. You won't be the last.*

Ezra exhaled. "We're not just up against lies."

"No," I said. "We're up against the architects of them."

And outside, under the veil of night, the firmament remained.

Waiting.

We cleared the coffee table and spread out every document, map, notebook, and fragment we had. The constellation chart Hargrave left us had seven points marked in red: seven dates, seven alignments. The first one was just two weeks away.

We cross-referenced the date with historical events and stumbled on a pattern. Each alignment Hargrave noted correlated with a shift—political, technological, or spiritual. The next one would fall on a lunar eclipse.

Ezra reached for Mason's notebook, flipping to a page labeled "Project Blue Beam?"

The page was wild—lines connecting ancient temples to broadcast towers, old star maps to news headlines. It looked like conspiracy soup. But then we saw it. A phrase circled three times: "They will simulate His return."

Goosebumps.

Ezra whispered, "They're going to counterfeit the Second Coming."

We sat in silence. Mason's final notes weren't about disproving space. They were about preparing hearts. "Not to prove the dome," I said quietly. "To withstand the lie."

Ezra nodded. "The countdown isn't about the sky. It's about the soul."

And from that moment on, we knew we weren't just decoding.

The next red mark on Hargrave's chart landed on a date that meant nothing to me—just a strange notation scrawled near the edge of one of the concentric rings. But Ezra recognized it. "It's an old feast day," he said, squinting at the ink like it might move. "One of the lesser ones. Barely observed anymore. You only see it mentioned in old liturgical calendars."

He pulled out a battered concordance, the kind with cracked binding and years of notes scribbled in the margins. We flipped through it together, searching through transliterations, root words, and cross-references. And then he found it. "The name," he murmured, tapping the page. "The Hebrew root look. It means 'illumination.'"

He paused as he looked again. "But it also means 'false light.'" Neither of us said anything for a long moment. The room felt quieter than it had a second ago. "We should be looking," Ezra finally said, "for something that imitates glory."

The days that followed felt like waiting for thunder. The date loomed quietly, but the world around us began to hum with something... off.

At first, it was scattered reports. A strange atmospheric shimmer seen by pilots over the Pacific. An observatory in Chile that lost its instruments to a sudden magnetic pulse, then quickly issued a public retraction that didn't explain anything. Lights over China, caught on cell phones, rising and vanishing like mirrored fire.

None of it made the front page, but the pattern was forming.

Ezra started keeping a notebook, tallying the details: Celestial flashes, Heat signatures with no origin, Static bleeding into broadcasts.

Then came the video. Grainy. Shaky. But unmistakable. A burning figure descending slowly through a sky choked with clouds, filmed from a crumbling balcony somewhere in Eastern Europe.

No one claimed the footage. No context. No source. Just thirty-seven seconds of silence and fire.

The divide came quickly. Some churches called it a sign, a visitation, a warning, a promise. Others cried deception, warning of a great delusion. The Vatican broke its silence three days before the marked date. They urged discernment, Caution, Prayer.

But for the first time, they didn't laugh.

Ezra looked up from his notes, his expression unreadable. "That," he said, "is when I got worried."

I stayed up that night watching the footage over and over. The figure wasn't detailed—just a shape—but there was something familiar in the way people responded. Not fear. Reverence. It mimicked the awe reserved for something sacred.

I opened my Bible. Revelation 13:13 stared back at me: *And he performed great signs, even causing fire to come down from heaven to the earth in full view of the people.*

I read it twice.

And then I wept.

Chapter Fourteen

We weren't alone. That became clear the day we met Jalen.

He was waiting in my classroom after school. Mid-thirties, clean-cut, with a worn Bible and eyes that looked like they'd seen things no one should have to carry.

"You don't know me," he said, "but I know what you're studying. And I know what's coming."

Ezra stepped in from the hallway, tense.

Jalen held up a small pendant—a cross wrapped in a braided leather cord. "They call us the Remnant. Not a cult. Not a club. Just believers who started seeing the cracks in the story and chose to remember."

He unrolled a canvas map—older than anything we'd seen. It showed the earth flat, the dome above, waters above and below. But what caught my eye was the seal at the bottom: a lion, a scroll, and the word *witness*. "This isn't theory," Jalen said. "It's memory. And it's coming back."

He stayed for hours, telling us stories passed down from his grandfather—who had once worked on classified radar projects. About strange readings, silent firings, and the day a man vanished mid-shift after asking why the stars didn't move like they should.

He handed us a copy of a translated Dead Sea scroll fragment. It read: *The heavens are fixed, but the lie is not.*

After Jalen left, the silence felt heavier. The kind of silence that asks more questions than it answers. Ezra paced while I took notes. "If what he said is true, then everything Mason warned about is accelerating. The alignments, the feasts, the broadcasts, none of it is random."

We pulled out every chart we had and laid them side by side. Hargrave's countdown. The Remnant's map. Mason's journal. And one thread kept emerging: convergence. A date, just a month away, marked by a rare celestial crossing—a moment where the sun, moon, and stars would align directly over the poles.

"They'll use it," I said.

Ezra nodded. "Blue Beam. Projected glory. Manufactured divinity. It'll look like fulfillment, but it's fabrication."

I closed my eyes and whispered, "Even the elect..."

We decided to travel.

If the next alignment would be over the poles, we needed someone who'd worked in polar observation. Jalen gave us a name—Margot Ellison. A former NOAA analyst who went dark five years ago after submitting a report titled *Optical Distortion and the Firmament Hypothesis*.

We packed bags that night, and Ezra locked up the map in the school's AV vault. We didn't know who was watching, but we knew they were close.

Too close.

Chapter Fifteen

We made it out of the city by nightfall. Ezra drove while I scanned the rearview mirror, half-expecting headlights that never came. We didn't tell anyone where we were going, not even Jalen. The scroll had pointed us toward a location in northern Georgia, the Appalachian foothills, just past an abandoned ranger station. It took us three hours and two wrong turns to find it. We didn't speak much, but the air between us was heavy with implication. The Remnant wasn't just a rumor. It had names. Faces. Locations.

What we found wasn't what I expected. No secret base. No metal hatch. Just a grove of cypress trees and a clearing surrounded by stone markers. At first, I thought it was a forgotten cemetery, until I realized the stones weren't graves. They were coordinates. Angled, engraved, etched with phrases in Latin, Greek, and Hebrew.

One stone stood at the center, taller than the rest. Ezra brushed off the moss to reveal a single line from Revelation 4:1: *"Behold, a door was opened in heaven."*

We circled the clearing. The place hummed—not with sound, but with presence. Ezra took out a compass. The needle spun wildly. "That's not magnetic disturbance," he said. "That's resonance."

We stood still, unsure of what to do next, when a woman stepped from the trees. She looked like a relic from another era—stoic, silver-haired, her eyes sharp behind wire-rimmed glasses. A Bible was tucked under one arm, a weathered satchel over the other. But her presence radiated both warning and welcome.

"You shouldn't be here," she said.

"We followed a map," I replied.

She studied us in silence, then nodded. "Margot Ellison. NOAA. Formerly."

Ezra extended his hand. "We've read your work."

She led us to a small stone shelter hidden behind the rise. Inside were journals, faded photographs, and instruments that looked older than the Cold War. She lit a lantern and pulled out a drawer labeled THRESHOLD ARRAY.

"What is it?" I asked.

"Not what," she said. "Where."

Margot explained that during the early days of atmospheric research, something was discovered—an anomaly in the stratosphere that repeated itself like clockwork over the poles. They called it the Threshold Array. But it wasn't natural.

"They weren't studying it," she said. "They were using it." She unrolled a diagram: concentric rings above a flat plane, intersected by towers. One tower bore the same emblem from Hargrave's scroll: a lion, a scroll, and a crown.

"It's a signal jammer," she explained. "But not for communication— spiritual resonance. It blocks frequencies. Sound, light, even memory."

Ezra leaned forward. "That's why they needed the fake sky. To mask the original frequencies."

I whispered, "To hide the voice of God."

Margot nodded. "The veil was never just atmospheric. It was engineered. And someone went to great lengths to ensure we forgot."

Margot's cabin wasn't just a shelter—it was a library, a war room, and a sanctuary for the hunted truth. We arrived exhausted, but what we found inside reignited our urgency. Everything was catalogued. She had weather reports, thermal imagery, eyewitness accounts, hand-copied pages from Enoch, Jasher, and Jubilees. She had Revelation memorized—and not the sanitized Sunday version. The raw, uncut scroll.

The word *veil* kept surfacing. "It's not just a metaphor," she told us. "They've engineered a literal filter between us and the heavens. Not outer space, the firmament. God's original dome. The one that still holds back the waters above."

Ezra frowned. "But who's 'they'?"

She pulled out a binder stamped with the initials 'O.S.I.'—Office of Strategic Influence. It had been defunct officially since the early 2000s, but the documents inside painted a deeper lineage: the British Tavistock Institute, DARPA, NASA, and something more ancient— occult orders that trace back to Babylon, Nimrod, and the Tower that was stopped by God Himself.

"They never stopped building," Margot said. "They just changed materials. From bricks and mortar to frequency and deception."

She showed us a NOAA logbook from her final polar assignment. One entry was circled in red: *Magneto-anomalous echo, polar crest, 2:17 a.m.*

"That's when they activated what I call the lattice net," she said. "Not a satellite. Not a telescope. A resonance grid. Invisible to the eye but structured like a mesh. It refracts truth. Dampens it. You can feel it when you pray, when you look up, when you ask questions they don't want asked."

She handed us a thermal photo showing the sky above the pole—a woven pattern glowing like veins. "They don't want you to know what's above us. Or Who."

Ezra was quiet. So was I. The silence wasn't fear—it was grief. We realized how much had been stolen.

That night, we climbed the ridge. Stars barely peeked through. The sky looked... artificial. And as I stood in that stillness, Genesis 1 came alive in me: *And God said, let there be a firmament in the midst of the waters...* I had read it a thousand times. But now it read me.

When we returned, Ezra prayed aloud. Not polished. Not rehearsed. Just: "Lord, give us eyes to see, and ears that won't close."

That night, I dreamed.

The dome trembled. Cracks of light opened like veins. And a voice, not mine, said: *You were born for such a time as this.*

Others arrived in small numbers: a woman in scrubs who once taught Sunday school, a retired linguist from Auburn, a father with two teenage sons who recited Psalms from memory. They came without phones. No names were exchanged beyond first ones. But they carried scrolls, fragments, photos, and pages of Scripture cross-referenced with cosmological charts.

One man showed a tattered map passed down from his grandfather—flat, circular, with Jerusalem at the center and an ice wall drawn thick along the edge.

"Every ancient civilization believed the same thing," he said. "A domed earth, pillars beneath, and waters above. What changed wasn't the earth—it was the agenda."

A woman quoted Job 26:7—*He stretcheth out the north over the empty place, and hangeth the earth upon nothing.*

"That doesn't mean it's floating in space," she said. "It means it's anchored, set in place by God, suspended in order—not chaos."

We stayed up late comparing notes, dreams, and convictions. I felt like a student again, only this time the curriculum wasn't mathematics—it was divine architecture, prophetic warning, and buried truth.

They explained how the Remnant had once been vast. Missionaries, historians, and pastors who spoke of the firmament without shame. But slowly, they were removed—discredited, labeled as fringe, or silenced altogether. Some vanished entirely.

"Seminaries shifted," Margot said. "They stopped teaching Hebrew cosmology. Called Genesis poetry. Downplayed Revelation. Said they were written using poetic language and imagery. They gave the church a soft sky."

That phrase stuck with me.

A soft sky.

We prayed together before sunrise, kneeling on the floor. The Spirit was thick. I didn't have words for what I felt, but I knew this: truth wasn't a theory. It was a Person. And He was calling us to remember what the world was made to forget.

When we left, we were no longer just survivors. We were witnesses. And the sky had not forgotten us.

Chapter Sixteen

We returned to town, changed. Every sound, every star, every moment of stillness now felt like a question demanding an answer. The countdown from Hargrave's chart was nearing another red date. A convergence predicted for the Feast of Trumpets. Ezra said it couldn't be coincidence.

Back in my apartment, we met with Jalen again. He brought blueprints and pages from ancient manuscripts, some recovered from a monastery that had burned mysteriously in 1983. "They're inverting everything," Jalen said. "Taking sacred patterns and flipping them. The festivals, the symbols, even the names."

Ezra pointed to one translation: *'In the latter days, they will call good evil and evil good.'*

I sat back and stared at our wall of clippings. The false light. The counterfeit descent. The fake stars. "This isn't just deception," I said. "It's ritual."

They were staging a false heaven to prevent people from reaching the real one. Ezra closed his eyes. "Project Blue Beam isn't just science fiction. It isn't just about surveillance or control. It's spiritual warfare. They are creating a counterfeit glory designed to draw worship away from the One who deserves it."

We mapped it all—ancient alignments, broadcast towers, cities built on ley lines. Every false thing had a counterpart, a shadow cast in defiance of something older, deeper, true.
It was all opposition. Intentional. The deception wasn't random, it was architectural. Strategic.

And in that moment, I understood something Mason had scribbled in the margin of his Bible: *Every lie is a blueprint for the truth it imitates.*

Two weeks before the celestial alignment, the world blinked. For seventeen seconds, every major screen went black. CNN. BBC. Fox. TikTok. Instagram. Phones froze. Stadium jumbotrons dimmed. Airport monitors flickered into darkness.

And then it appeared.

A glowing triangle with an eye at its center. Iris dilated, unblinking, slowly rotating against a backdrop of static. Slowly rotating. Silent. No words. No logos. No disclaimers.

Just the eye.

Then came the tone. It was low and harmonic, almost sacred, but there was something wrong with it. It reverberated in my bones, like a hymn, but played in reverse as if holiness had bent back on itself. Beneath the surface, I could hear whispers layered into the frequency. An old language, not in any modern language known to man. It sounded like a stone remembering the chisel. Like fire recalling the first breath of air.

Ezra replayed the track on a loop, slowing down the tempo. "Ancient tongues," he said eyes wide, "Known only by those who remembered Babel."

People called it a cyberattack, a breach, or a hijacking. But deep inside, we knew this was the fifth seal. Not a war. Not a plague. Not yet.

Just a silence so loud it unsettled even the skeptics. "They're mimicking Revelation," Margot whispered. "But their messiah isn't the Lamb. It's the image."

The weight of it landed hard. Not just symbolism. Not just imitation. Blasphemy: strategic, systemic, rehearsed.

The war had turned spiritual. Everyone felt it, even if they couldn't name it. A strange stillness spread across the world. Not peace, pause.

Churches filled and emptied in equal measure. Some wept. Some walked away.

A pastor in Ohio was arrested for refusing to remove a banner that read: "We will not worship the image." Another in Nairobi disappeared after declaring on live stream, "This is not the tribulation. This is the test."

The Remnant began to stir. That night around midnight, Jalen arrived with news from the underground. Across the movement, pastors were abandoning their notes and turning to fire.

Revelation, line by line. No skipping. No allegory or imagery. No spiritualized metaphors to blunt the blade. One church in the hills of Tennessee painted Scripture across its concrete walls:
The heavens declare the glory of God; the skies proclaim the work of His hands.

Another, in an abandoned subway tunnel in Berlin, was reciting Psalm 2 nightly by candlelight:
Why do the nations rage...The kings of the earth set themselves, and the rulers take counsel together...

They weren't studying anymore. They were preparing. The fifth seal was never about mass death. It was about who would stand when the silence hit.

The martyrs in Revelation don't cry out during chaos. They cry out in stillness, under the altar, unseen, unheard by the world.

Ezra said it best: "This is the part where the faithful look around and realize... we're alone. The crowd's gone. The applause is gone. And now we find out who's actually willing to die for the Word."

We debated going public.

"They'll come for you," Ezra warned.

"They're already coming," I said. "Might as well speak before they silence us."

We recorded from Margot's front room. No editing. No frills. Just a blackboard, a Bible, and a shaking hand.

I read Genesis 1, then Job 37:18 — *Hast thou with him spread out the sky, which is strong, and as a molten looking glass?*

I showed them ancient maps. Flat. Domed. Consistent. I asked why, if we were on a spinning ball, Polaris never moved. Why water finds its level. Why no camera has shown the stars beyond the dome. I held up the Bible and said, "If this is true, then everything else is a lie. And you were made for more."

Then we prayed and posted it through the Remnant relay.

Chapter Seventeen

They came before sunrise. No knocks. No warrants. No questions. Just three black SUVs speeding into the gravel driveway. No license plates or insignia. Masked men with tactical gear. Government? Private contractors? We never found out.

Margot had drills. Ezra and Jalen were already moving before the doors shut behind them. I dropped to the ground and crawled toward the back of the property, my heart pounding, and lungs burning. The rain barrel under the pine trees was half-rotted, but it hid me. I curled into the damp earth, pulling leaves over my boots. I held my breath until my vision swam.

Boots crunched past. Once. Then again. A pause and a whisper on a comm.
And then...nothing.

They didn't take Ezra.

They didn't take Jalen.

They didn't take me.

They took Margot.

We waited until sundown to approach the cabin, making sure the men had gone. Smoke was drifting from the chimney, but it wasn't wood. The door had been left ajar, hanging crooked on a single hinge. Etched into the splintered wood, not painted, not carved, but scorched, were four words:

SPEECH IS A CHOICE.

Inside, it looked like a ritual of erasure. Her shelves emptied. Her books torn and half-burned in the fireplace. Her computers cracked open like ribcages. Hard drives shattered. Wires yanked out by the roots. The Remnant chart gone. No prints. No blood. No trail. Just the unmistakable absence of truth.

Jalen stood in the doorway; his jaw clenched; eyes fixed on the scorched message. "She was marked," he said.

Ezra nodded slowly, almost mechanically. "They're targeting the voices now. Not the loudest just the clearest."

Outside, the wind picked up. And somewhere in the distance, we heard the low hum of that tone again, just long enough to remind us: We were still being watched.

I dropped to my knees beside her fireplace, the ashes were still warm. My fingers sank into them staining my hands. I had waited too long. The message had gone out but so had the enemy. And now the woman who had once carried the clearest voice among us was gone.

Ezra came and stood beside me; hand outstretched holding a scroll. It was worn, frayed, ancient. From one of Jalen's contacts in the underground, smuggled out of a sealed library beneath the ruins of Smyrna. A creed that had been hand-copied by the persecuted church of the second century. The ink was faded, but the words felt alive. Fierce. Unshakable. Eternal.

It read: *We do not fear the flames, for truth cannot burn. We do not fear the silence, for God still speaks. We will not bow to the lie, nor serve its image.*

I read it again. And again. Until the words buried themselves in my bones. Until the fire in Margot's hearth became something holy. She was gone. But her voice? It was just getting started.

We lit a candle that night. One flame. One truth. And I knew: this war wasn't about knowledge. It was about remembrance. And we had only just begun.

Word spread faster than we wanted. A leak, maybe. Or someone listening. Either way, we started noticing strange cars, new substitute teachers, and unfamiliar faces in familiar places.

Ezra and I went underground, figuratively and literally. An old storm shelter beneath the church where Mason used to go became our war room. We encrypted our files, left decoys, changed SIM cards.

It wasn't paranoia. It was preservation.

The Remnant network expanded not just in numbers but in depth. They came from across the fractured world: farmers with dirt under their nails and prophecy in their pockets. Retired pilots who had seen things at 30,000 feet they were never allowed to report. Pastors who had walked away from pulpits too polished to preach truth. Cartographers with ancient maps inked by trembling hands. Linguists chasing the root of words they swore had been erased. Seminary dropouts who had stopped studying doctrine and started living it.

They came with pieces of the puzzle and warnings. "They're accelerating the deception," one man said. "Using predictive programming in media, signals in the grid, even manipulated dreams. The war isn't just for your mind. It's for your memory."

My voice broke as she read a report: *Simulated descent observed over Cairo. Reported as a 'Messiah manifestation.' Thousands knelt. Authorities silent.*

I didn't finish the next line; I didn't have to. It had begun. Not just the spectacle, but the surrender. The real sky still waited, untouched, but the counterfeit was being worshiped.

We stood under the heavens, night after night, watching, waiting. Not for signs, but asking for discernment, for endurance, for the courage to remember what they told us to forget.

The stars pulsed back. Faint, distant, steady. Not with answers. But with invitation.

Chapter Eighteen

The church basement had no windows, just stone walls and thick air. Ezra rigged a ventilation fan from the old baptistry closet and I borrowed folding tables and chairs from the fellowship hall. It wasn't glamorous, but it was safe.

We used butcher paper to draw the timelines: biblical, astronomical, political. Three strands that shouldn't have matched. But they did. Over and over again. Hargrave's chart had triggered something, like a decoder ring for the last thousand years of deception. The alignments weren't random. They were rehearsals. False signs tied to false saviors.

Ezra found a passage from Daniel that hadn't struck us before. *"He will honor a god of fortresses—a god unknown to his ancestors; he will deal with the strongest fortresses with the help of a foreign god."*

"Fortresses," he said, circling the word. "What if it's not military at all? What if it's broadcast towers?"

We'd already tracked some of them—abandoned Cold War antennas, pseudo-cell towers that emitted no signal, dishes aimed not outward, but up. Frequencies, not firepower. And suddenly, Daniel's words took on new meaning.

Jalen returned that evening with a tattered leather-bound book. He laid it gently on the table like it was sacred. Inside were sermons written in 1917 by a rural pastor who had preached that the sky was solid and sacred—and that the end would come when men tried to pierce it.

"He died in prison," Jalen said quietly. "For refusing to denounce it."

We didn't speak for a while. Because the deeper we dug, the clearer it became: They weren't just trying to keep us from seeing the real sky. They were trying to become it.

We spent the next week tracing what Jalen called convergence events—times in history where natural phenomenon, staged events, and spiritual deception aligned. The launch of Sputnik. The televised moon landing. The 2012 "awakening." Even events like Y2K, which had no physical consequence but left millions spiritually frayed, caught between expectation and collapse.

"It's mass rehearsal," Ezra said as he flipped through decades of headlines. "Dress rehearsals for delusion."

The more we looked, the clearer the pattern became. Every few decades: awe, fear, confusion. A global heartbeat reset. Each one preparing the world for something bigger, something more convincing.

We returned to the Dead Sea scroll fragment, hand copied, faded but legible. *The heavens are fixed, but the lie is not.*

I stared at those words like they were the heartbeat of everything we'd uncovered. The stars hadn't changed. The skies still proclaimed the glory of God. But our instruments had been tampered with and our filters changed. Our textbooks rewritten, our translations diluted, our telescopes pointed just slightly away from what mattered.

It wasn't just about astronomy. It was about authority. Who had the right to name the heavens, to define what we saw, and dictate what we believed.

The remnant grew in number and caution. We now communicated through couriers and ciphered email threads as we could no longer rely on open threads. Some members had dreams that confirmed specific passages of Scripture with frightening clarity. Others brought ancient maps, pre-Columbus star charts, forgotten Jewish commentaries that never treated the firmament as poetry, but as something solid, real, and unbroken.

Then came the broadcast.

It hijacked every frequency: every channel, every phone, every screen, even radios that hadn't worked in years came to life. It started out like an emergency alert. But instead of a warning, it was a declaration. A being of light appeared over Jerusalem framed by clouds that pulsed with unnatural color. Its presence flickered across every screen on earth. Then it spoke. The voice echoed in every language at once, not through translation, but understood. Direct. Undeniable.

It spoke peace.

It spoke unity.

It spoke control.

And people worshipped.

Ezra grabbed my hand, trembling. "Revelation thirteen," he said barely above a whisper. "Signs and lying wonders."

I don't know why I stayed behind. Maybe I needed the silence. Or maybe I was afraid that once I said it out loud, it would all be real.

It's quiet now and the room is empty, but my hands are still shaking from what we saw in the field. The shimmer. The stars breathing. The veil. Ezra called it prophecy. I called it impossible...until it wasn't.

I sit in the corner of the church basement, knees pulled to my chest, Hargrave's chart unrolled beside me. I trace the constellations, but I'm not studying them. I'm... *listening*. Because something has changed. For the first time, I realized, this isn't about science, evidence, or proving anything to anyone. It's about remembering something I've always known but had buried deep under facts and fear.

I didn't stop believing when my mother died. I just... stopped looking.

Grief didn't hit me like a storm. It crept in like fog; quiet and dense, softening everything until even God seemed distant. Faded.

She used to talk about Him like He was closer than breath. Like His voice was in the stars, and His fingerprints could still be found in our atmosphere if we just knew where to look. She'd sing as she cooked, quote Psalms while folding laundry.

I used to roll my eyes. But deep down... it made me feel safe.

When the diagnosis came, and the months bled into hospice visits, and prayers turned into silence, I stopped looking. Not because I didn't want to believe, but because I was afraid of what I'd find if I did.

So, I buried God beside her and then buried myself in logic, in math, in data. Control and certainty felt safer than surrender. But tonight...tonight I saw the sky shimmer. I saw stars pulse like heartbeats and clouds rest against a veil we weren't supposed to remember. I felt something ancient stir in my soul. And I broke.

The Bible lies open beside me on the cold basement floor, Psalm 19 circled in pencil. I rest my hand on the page and close my eyes.

"God..." My voice catches. The name tastes unfamiliar. "...I'm so sorry, I buried you with her. But I know now, you didn't stay buried."

A whisper, a crack, the beginning. "I ran from You when I needed You most. I let silence speak louder than truth. I thought forgetting would keep me safe." Tears start to slide down my cheeks, hot against the chill in the air. "I don't know how to come back. I don't know how to believe again, but I want to."

I sit in the stillness, waiting. No vision. No thunder. But something inside me softens. Not certainty. Not resolution. Invitation. And maybe that's how grace begins.

Footsteps echo down the stairs behind me. I don't look up. I don't need to. Ezra crouches beside me and sets a thermos near my feet. "Coffee," he says. "Not very good, but it's warm."

I manage a small smile. "Thanks."

He doesn't ask what I'm doing on the floor with a Bible open and tears drying on my cheeks. He just nods, eyes kind. "We need you," he says. Not pressure. Not flattery. Just truth.

I glance back at the page. Psalm 19. *"Day after day they pour forth speech; night after night they reveal knowledge."*

Then I stand slowly, brushing dust from my hands. "I think I'm ready," I say then pause. "No, scratch that. I'm not ready. But I am done pretending this isn't real."

Ezra nods once. "Good. Because it's just beginning."

I nodded in agreement, tears brimming not out of fear, but in grief because I knew how I had forsaken the truth for so long. And know that even now, few still remembered the truth. So many had traded the voice of the Shepherd for the glow of the screen. So many had mistaken light for glory. Wonder for holiness.

There was only one way forward now. We had to expose the veil. And we had to do it soon. Before the next sign appeared.

Chapter Nineteen

The fallout from the broadcast was immediate.

Churches split overnight. Entire communities, once united by beliefs or tradition, fractured. Some hailed the being as divine, calling it the long-awaited return, the fulfilment of prophesy. While others scrambled to explain it away with science or silence, a psyop, hologram, mass hysteria. The Vatican released a cautious statement urging discernment but offered no denial. Evangelical leaders went live to disagree with each other. Different denominations unraveled on air. The media called it the dawn of a new spiritual age. A global awakening, cosmic convergence, a post doctrinal revelation.

But we knew better. It wasn't the true return; it was the enthronement of a lie. A false light wearing sacred language like camouflage. The world had seen a sign and fallen to its knees. But not us, we had seen the pattern before, and we remembered the warning.

Ezra met me in the church basement just after dusk. The power was out again, and we lit the room with oil lamps and the last working flashlight we had left. Shadows danced across the old stone walls, flickering like ghosts of past revivals.

He was already there, hunched over a table scarred by decades of prayer meetings and potlucks, his Bible open to Matthew 24. He didn't greet me. He just read. His voice echoed through the quiet like a warning from the deep:

"Then if anyone says to you, 'Look, here is the Messiah!' or 'There he is!' do not believe it. For false messiahs and false prophets will appear and perform great signs and wonders to deceive, if possible, even the elect. See, I have told you ahead of time. So, if anyone tells you, 'There he is, out in the wilderness,' do not go out; or 'Here he is, in the inner rooms,' do not believe it. For as lightning that comes from the east is visible even in the west, so will be the coming of the Son of Man."

The words landed with the weight of truth: sharp, immovable, a boundary line drawn across the spirit. "It won't be secret," I said. "It won't need an announcement."

He let the words settle, closed the Bible slowly, then finally looked at me and nodded. And it won't require interpretation."

We sat in silence, and for a moment, I could feel the weight of every false gospel falling around us: the videos, the broadcasts, the glowing apparitions in the sky. How convincing they'd been. How many had already knelt.

The real coming of Christ wouldn't be filtered through satellites or framed by subtitles. It would break the sky wide open. It would be terrible, unmistakable, undeniable and unstoppable. Glory, not projection. Fire, not flash.

We gathered the remnant that night. Word had gone out across the encrypted channels. Some walked for hours to get there. Others came underground—through back alleys, through forests, through tunnels no longer mapped. They came not with confidence, but with conviction.

There were about seventeen of us in all. Some were old, faces like folded parchment, hands that trembled when they lit the candles. Others were barely grown, teenagers with wiry frames and fire in their eyes. But every one of us had seen through the broadcast. Had refused the image. Had remembered.

We laid our tools out on the table: Handwritten scrolls sealed in wax. Pre-Columbus star maps marked with realigned constellations. Crumpled paper journals from missionaries who died unnamed. Dreams recorded in trembling handwriting. Scriptures with notes scribbled in margins, worn by fingers and tears.

Jalen stood at the head of the room, holding a leather-bound book he'd recovered from the ruins of a church burned in the uprisings—pages warped by heat, but still legible. When he spoke, it wasn't loud. It didn't need to be. "Every time the enemy has built a tower; God has torn it down. This time, they've built it out of light. Pixels. Satellites. Data. Deception stitched into the sky. But the lie is no less fragile."

He looked around the room, and no one spoke. Not because we were afraid, because we were resolved.

I looked at the faces around me. Margot's seat sat empty, but her presence hung in the air like a psalm still echoing after the music has stopped. A teenager clutched a sealed envelope, her latest decoded transmission from a Remnant cell in South America. A former seminary professor was sketching out biblical timelines on parchment by hand, whispering Scripture as he wrote. Two farmers from Kansas had brought jars of oil and laminated maps of star alignments they swore hadn't changed in 400 years. A boy no older than thirteen held a shoebox full of transistor parts and a notebook of ciphered hymns.

We were scattered no longer. We were threads drawn back to the center, knotted together by truth the world had tried to erase. The world called us radical. Dangerous. Misguided. But we had remembered what they were made to forget.

Ezra looked at me then, and I knew what he was thinking. The next convergence wasn't theoretical anymore. It was days away. The signs were lining up—on the ground, in the heavens, in the hearts of men.

We would meet it head-on. Not with weapons. Not with platforms. But with the truth. Ancient, unfiltered, and uncompromised.

We had one mission now: To expose the veil before the next deception took root. Before millions more knelt. Before the sky was rewritten forever.

Chapter Twenty

We didn't sleep that night.

Instead, we prayed. Long, aching prayers that felt like they stretched beyond the ceiling and pressed through the veil. We recited Scripture aloud—Psalms, Revelation, Isaiah. Anything that reminded us of the truth that had already been written. Ezra read aloud from Isaiah 44: *"I am the LORD, who made all things, who alone stretched out the heavens, who spread out the earth by myself."*

It anchored us.

By morning, the group began to divide. Not in disagreement—but in assignment. We couldn't stay hidden any longer. Some were tasked with compiling the evidence—photos, translations, satellite overlays, and the coded messages from Hargrave. Others would take them to key churches, homeschool co-ops, and pastors they trusted. The rest of us would prepare for the next event.

The next convergence would be visible from the southern hemisphere, centered over Antarctica—home of more secrets than even the archives could contain. The maps confirmed it. The ancient star charts, the atmospheric readings, the frequency echoes. They all pointed to the ice, a place colder than space, where silence wasn't just a condition but a strategy.

It made sense. Antarctica was where signals went to disappear. Where sensors failed and truth froze before it could be spoken. That's where the coordinates ended, and Margot's last trail stopped.

Her last known upload had referenced ancient polar anomalies, reflections in the firmament, and a chilling footnote from an 1840s missionary journal: *"The heavens here press low, as if watching."*

We hadn't heard from her since the raid. She never escaped. But maybe her work did. And if so, someone needed to find it.

Jalen would go find her. He volunteered without hesitation. He packed his gear and Margot's last notes into his jacket. I could tell by looking in his eyes this wasn't about a mission, it was about finishing what she started.

Before Jalen left, I hugged him tightly, whispering, "Come back with whatever she left behind."

Ezra and I stayed behind to prepare the local broadcast. We weren't going to expose a global deception on our own. That wasn't the assignment. Our job was to shine enough light to make someone, somewhere, question the dark.

We would launch a local broadcast during the convergence not a declaration, but an interruption.
A ripple in the illusion.

Shortwave Scripture. Analog signal bursts. Voice recordings layered with decoded scroll fragments and unrevised star charts.

We didn't need to be loud. We just needed to be true. Because the lie was powerful, but it was also brittle.

Truth doesn't have to shout to be heard. It just has to survive.

Jalen left under cover of night. No one saw him off at the airstrip not because we didn't care, but because invisibility was safety now. The small transport had been arranged through one of the Remnant's last safe contacts in the aviation sector, a retired cargo pilot who no longer asked questions, only coordinates.

From there, it was a patchwork journey: Civilian airports. Unmarked aircraft. A supply vessel rerouted under a falsified manifest. And finally, the silence of the ice.

Antarctica.

Even the name sounded final. There were no roads. No noise. No margin for error. Just wind, ice, and a sky that looked older than time.

Jalen stepped off the final transport with only a pack, a worn copy of the Psalms, and a satphone that might stop working the moment he needed it most.

The cold hit differently here. It didn't bite; it buried. Not just flesh, but thought, conviction, breath. He was utterly alone. But not abandoned.

He followed the coordinates encoded in Margot's last known data dump, buried beneath a verse from Job: *"Have you entered the storehouses of the snow, or seen the storehouses of the hail, which I reserve for times of trouble?"*

Each coordinate led deeper inland, beyond research stations, beyond mapped terrain. Toward something forgotten on purpose.

Three days in, the weather turned. Visibility dropped. The wind howled like a warning.
But the compass kept spinning, a magnetized refusal to guide. That night, Jalen found shelter in a natural ice cavern—its entrance half-covered by snowdrift. He built a fire from chemical fuel, pressed his back against the icy wall, and listened.

Not for danger, but for silence. Because that's what Margot had written in her final margin: "When you're close, the silence will shift. Not louder. Not quieter. Just... intentional."

The cold had stopped feeling like cold. It was something else now. Something deeper. On the fifth day, he found it. A crevice marked only by a rusted pole and a symbol etched into the rock:

א𐤉𐤀𐤆

YHWH. Ancient Hebrew, untouched by digital hands.

Jalen moved carefully through the collapsed corridor, his boots crunching over ancient frost and fractured stone. The drone had gone silent five minutes ago, likely interference from the magnetic spike they'd been tracking. He was alone now, the signal patchy, the light from his headlamp flickering in rhythm with something he didn't understand.

The tunnel shouldn't have existed. The readings he was picking up were impossible. And yet... here it was.

He descended through the breach down into the glacier wall, where ancient stone jutted from the ice like ribs from a long-buried corpse. Not chiseled. Not quarried. Grown, as if the structure had risen through command, not construction. The air was thinner here. Older.

Jalen passed through a narrow arch and froze.

The chamber beyond opened like a cathedral—circular, domed, impossibly vast. Ice dripped from a high ceiling laced with crystal veins. And in the center of the room, sprawled in a shallow basin of ice and sediment, was a skeleton.

No. A being. The skull alone was nearly the size of a man's torso. Its eye sockets were cavernous, and the jaw was fractured; shattered from the inside out. The ribcage arched unnaturally high, and the femurs, though partially embedded in frost, stretched well beyond human proportions.

He counted six fingers on one of the exposed hands. Beside the remains lay what looked like a weapon, or what used to be part of one. Bronze, maybe. Scorched. Etched with symbols that glowed faintly when his light passed over them.

Not Hebrew.
Not Greek.
Older.

Jalen exhaled slowly, his breath fogging in front of him. Every instinct told him to retreat. But something in his chest, a pressure he hadn't felt since childhood, pushed him forward.

At the far end of the chamber, behind the remains, he found it. A sealed alcove. Carved into the wall: a star-map. Constellations no longer recognized by modern charts. Below it: a smooth platform, and upon it a crate sealed in wax and cloth.

Wrapped in linen. Sealed in blackened wax. Resting atop a slab of stone etched with a phrase he recognized from Hargrave's early translations: "And the Watchers fell through flame,
and their bones cried out from the earth. Bury them, lest the sky remember."

His hands trembled as he reached for the scroll. Not from fear. Not from cold. From weight. Jalen bowed his head. Not in mourning, in reverence. He didn't know if he could make it back. Didn't know if the satphone would hold. Didn't know if the Remnant would still be broadcasting by the time he did.

But he had found what they needed and that was enough. He packed the crate, closed his coat, and turned back once, just once, looking again at the being in the ice. Its mouth was open. Not in agony. But in warning.

Then he stepped back into the white silence, not knowing if the next sound he'd hear would be the wind...or the veil beginning to tear.

Chapter Twenty-One

Two days later, just past midnight, the sky cracked.

Not in thunder—but in vision.

We were standing in the field behind the church with the rest of the remnant. No one spoke, not out loud anyway. The stars above us pulsed in strange rhythm, like someone holding their breath. The air felt heavy, charged, but alive. Ezra's hands shook as he adjusted the signal booster on the makeshift projector. A Frankenstein like contraption held together with duct tape, salvaged lenses, and desperation.

Then we saw it.

A shimmer, like glass under stress, stretched across the heavens. It was subtle at first. We wouldn't have noticed, if we weren't waiting in expectation. The firmament wasn't breaking, but it was being revealed. The light bent oddly, and where the clouds should have passed freely, they seemed to rest against something unseen. Something solid.

We recorded what we could, even as our screens glitched and reset. Technology failed, but it didn't matter. The people with eyes to see, they felt it. Scripture spoke of signs in the heavens, and now, the signs were undeniable. Tangible and breathing.

A child in the group pointed up and said, "It looks like it's breathing."

And it did. Ezra opened his Bible and read from Revelation 6:14, *"The sky receded like a scroll, rolling up..."*

For a moment, I felt something ancient stir. Not fear. Expectation.

The veil had not fallen, but it had trembled.

And no matter what happened next, the world could no longer pretend it wasn't there.

The following morning brought no headlines. No press conferences with NASA suits pointing at charts. No scientific explanations. There was no mention of the shimmer on any official feeds. No grainy footage leaked online. No frantic TikTok's or Reddit threads. Just silence. The sky had cracked open, or at least whispered that it could, and the world acted as though it hadn't heard a thing. But the silence itself was telling.

Ezra and I sat at the church's old folding table, surrounded by scribbled notes, still frames, cracked phones, and half-drunk coffee gone cold. The sanctuary, once meant for Sunday services, had become our war room. A battleground of truth and data.

His laptop glowed dimly in front of him, looping the same segment of footage over and over. Static flickered. The shimmer appeared and then quickly disappeared. The exact same frames, every time. It was as if the sky itself had edited the moment out.

"They scrubbed it," Ezra muttered, eyes bloodshot, voice low. "Live feeds, satellites, even private drones. Something's intercepting and corrupting anything that captures the veil."

I didn't ask how he knew. I'd stopped asking things like that weeks ago.

He sat back and rubbed his temple. "They've built a firewall around the sky."

I swallowed hard, unsure whether it was the caffeine or the truth curdling in my stomach. "Then what we saw..."

He nodded slowly. "It wasn't a glitch. It was a message." And then, almost as an afterthought, he whispered, "Someone... or something... doesn't want the world to see."

I nodded slowly. "Which means...they were watching too."

We weren't the only ones who'd seen it.

That afternoon, Jalen finally made contact.

His last known coordinates had pinged weeks ago, somewhere near the Antarctic exclusion zone—one of the few places left on Earth where signals go to die. We'd assumed the worst. Silence, even from Jalen, felt like the new normal.

But he hadn't spoken. Not directly. It was too risky, and he would've known that. Instead, a courier arrived, grimy from days of overland travel, with a sealed drive and a single sheet of lined paper folded inside. The ink was smudged, but the handwriting was unmistakably Jalen's.

"The ice doesn't lie. The horizon bends, but it doesn't curve. And the firmament echoes in ways radar can't explain. They built stations here to hide it—not study it. You must act before the next pass."

Ezra read it aloud once, then again, his voice flattening into something between awe and dread. He inserted the drive into his laptop. The screen blinked, then filled with cascading files, layers of sonar returns, radio signatures, atmospheric distortion. And then... the radar images.

Still frames, grayscale and ghostly. A sequence, timestamped and undeniable. A perfect arc: transparent, colossal, and rising from beyond the ice shelf. Not a cloud. Not a mirage. Something structural.

It looked like the edge of a dome. Not metaphor. Not theology. It was Geometry.

Ezra leaned closer. "Triangulated from three sources. It's not an anomaly. It's anchored."

My pulse spiked. "You mean... it's part of the terrain?"

He nodded once, slowly. "It's not in the sky. It *is* the sky."

The weight of that landed on my chest like stone.

"Genesis wasn't poetic," I whispered. "It was technical." And for the first time since this all began; I didn't just believe it. I knew it.

Chapter Twenty-Two

That night, Ezra stood at the pulpit of the small church. We didn't livestream. We didn't advertise. But word had spread. People filled every pew—some believers, some skeptics, some just desperate for something that rang true.

He opened his Bible to Job 37 and began to read *"He spreads out the skies like a mirror of cast bronze."*

The room stilled. The rustling of paper stilled. Even the sky outside seemed to hold its breath.

"There's been a war on that sky for centuries," Ezra said. "Not because it doesn't matter, but because it does. Because it testifies. Because it reminds us, we are not cosmic accidents, but crafted beings beneath a Creator's dome."

I watched the room—people leaning in, eyes glistening, questions flickering. They weren't here for entertainment. They were here for truth.

"We've forgotten," he continued. "Not just the shape of the world, but the shape of our faith. The structure. The urgency. The design."

Then he reached beneath the pulpit and pulled out the constellation chart, the one from Hargrave's sealed archive. Yellowed. Folded. Nearly torn at the edges. "And now... the countdown continues."

He pointed to the final red mark. Ezra paused, letting the silence stretch before the weight of his next words. "The date marked on this chart... the final alignment—it falls on the Feast of Trumpets," he said. "Yom Teruah."

A whisper moved through the room. Few understood and fewer still knew why it mattered.

"It's not a coincidence," he continued. "It never was. Nothing about this sky was ever random." He stepped out from behind the pulpit and held the constellation chart in one hand, the Bible in the other.

"The Feast of Trumpets marks the beginning of the Hebrew civil year. Prophetically, it signals something far greater. It's the day of *awakening blasts*, a divine alarm clock, shaking the world awake before judgment falls. It's the only feast that begins with the sighting of the new moon meaning," he turned, pointing toward the projector screen, "*no one knows the day or the hour*... until they see the sign."

A hush swept the room. "Sound familiar?"

A few nodded. A few wept.

Ezra flipped to 1 Thessalonians 4:16 and read: *"For the Lord Himself will descend from heaven with a shout, with the voice of an archangel, and with the trumpet of God..."*

He looked up. "The *last trumpet*, Paul said. That wasn't poetic either."

He pointed again to the red mark on the chart which was seven days away. It fell on the Feast of Trumpets. The ancient day when trumpets were sounded to call the assembly, to warn of war, and to announce a king.

"And so, I ask you," Ezra said, eyes scanning the faces before him, "When the veil opens, when the sky splits, when the heavens declare, what do you think they'll be announcing?"

The room held its breath. No one reached for their phones. No one whispered or shuffled. For the first time in what felt like months, people sat still, not distracted, not divided, not numbed.

Awake.

Ezra lowered the chart. The candles at the front of the sanctuary flickered with the weight of the moment. Behind him, the wooden cross on the wall stood stark and silent, like a shadow of something ancient and real enough to split the sky.

"This is not about fear," he said. "It's about readiness." Then he stepped down from the pulpit and walked to the center aisle, voice softer now, more human. "The Feast of Trumpets is a summons. A cry to repent. A call to gather. A warning to watch the skies. One week from tonight, the trumpet will sound, whether the world hears it or not."

A single chair creaked as someone shifted in the back row. Another person bowed their head to pray. Ezra looked to me just briefly. The kind of glance that asks, *Are we sure we're ready for this?*

I wasn't. But we were going anyway. He closed the Bible, not with finality, but with reverence.

The gathering ended without music. Without a benediction. Just quiet shuffling feet and solemn nods. A few stayed behind, unwilling to step back into a world that still pretended the sky hadn't spoken.

Afterwards, a woman approached us, mid-forties, eyes fierce, clutching a faded journal. She introduced herself as Lydia. Her grandfather had served in the early NASA communications corps. Before he died, he left behind pages of what she'd dismissed as madness—drawings of firmaments, references to Enoch, and a phrase repeated again and again: *"He who controls the sky, controls the narrative."*

I looked at Ezra.

We had heard those exact words from Mason. And now, with every hour that passed, it was becoming undeniable. The veil was weakening. The elect were awakening. The lie, though still loud, was losing ground to the whisper of truth.

Chapter Twenty-Three

Jalen's last message came in fragments.

A scrambled signal bounced through three relays—barely decipherable. Static, code words, and one clear phrase: *"I found the gate."*

Ezra replayed the audio again and again, slowing it down, isolating the waveform peaks. "If he's alive," he said, "they're hunting him."

We had a rough idea of where Jalen had gone—the location Margot left note of was just west of the Shackleton Range, deep in the Antarctic interior. The area had been listed off-limits by most international treaties, but it wasn't just about preservation. subtle, but consistent. It always hovered over the same narrow ridge, never fully settling, never fully dispersing. Like something beneath the ice was shifting space itself.

Hargrave's map had labeled that area as Sheol's Mirror. We'd assumed it was metaphorical. Symbolic. A reference to death or descent. Boy we were wrong

Two days later, a military drone feed leaked through an anonymous burner account. No caption. No timestamp. Just seven minutes of raw, silent footage.

What it showed made the room go cold.

An outpost, old, rust-streaked, likely predating the first UN treaties. Satellite domes half-buried in snow. Camouflaged towers stretched like skeletal fingers toward the pale sky. The site was silent, dormant... but not abandoned.

And near the ridge—a depression in the ice. Vast. Circular. Undisturbed. Not carved by machinery. Not shaped by weather.

It was too perfect, too symmetrical, like it was deliberate.

Ezra paused the video and overlaid Hargrave's celestial chart. The ancient constellation lines, the ones everyone had dismissed as mystical ramblings were aligned with the perimeter exactly. Every angle matched.

He leaned forward, whispering like he didn't want the room to hear: "This is it. The threshold."

Not a place. A mechanism, a convergence point where frequency, resonance, and magnetic distortion began to tear at the veil. Not to destroy it, just to weaken it. A place designed to reveal what lay above. Or worse...who might be waiting to come through.

The church basement had become a war room. Maps lined every wall. Passages of Scripture were taped alongside surveillance images. Psalm 148. Job 26. Revelation 4. All describing a heaven that was not some far-off realm, but an architecture above us.

Ezra pointed to a passage in Isaiah: *"Lift up your eyes on high and see: who created these? He who brings out their host by number..."*

"They don't want us lifting our eyes," he said. "Because when we do, we remember."

Outside, strange clouds hovered again. They were stationary, geometric, casting no shadows. We watched them with quiet reverence and quiet dread. Were they part of the unveiling... or the deception?

That night, I couldn't sleep. I dreamed of the dome again. But this time, I wasn't beneath it. I was inside it. It was like I was being held in a palm turned skyward. The stars above me weren't distant; they were ordered. Moving with purpose. And in the center of it all, a voice echoed: *"He alone stretches out the heavens and treads on the waves of the sea."*

I woke in tears. Because I finally understood the firmament wasn't just structure, it was promise, and it was breaking open.

Chapter Twenty-Four

The second appearance came without warning.

Just after dusk, phones across the globe lit up again. This time, the being hovered above New York, Rio, Cairo, Tokyo. Cities froze. Traffic halted. People dropped to their knees in public squares, but something was different.

This time, we were ready.

In the church basement, we had our systems primed. Ezra had rerouted the signals through an old HAM radio rig and a tangled mess of analog converters, scavenged hard drives, and duct-taped cables humming with low static. The walls were lined with foil insulation, not for temperature but interference. Everything down here buzzed with urgency.

We were watching the news feed when the image cut in. Sudden, crystalline, and deeply wrong. A figure of radiant light descended through the clouds; arms outstretched like a heavenly shepherd. Golden robes shimmered. The sky behind him glowed unnaturally. Birds circled above him in perfect rhythm, like something choreographed.

"He speaks of peace," Ezra muttered. "He performs signs."

"And he demands allegiance," I added, pointing to the scroll of text along the bottom of the screen. *'He comes to unify the faiths. All must align under the light.'*

It wasn't subtle anymore. This wasn't suggestion, it was a declaration.

Ezra flipped through Mason's journal, landing on a taped passage. "Revelation 13:13. *'He performs great signs, even causing fire to come down from heaven...'*" He looked at me. "We're watching prophecy play out."

We shifted into action.

The counter-broadcast we'd prepared wasn't flashy. It was Scripture, plain and unvarnished. Bible verses flashed alongside diagrams from Hargrave's celestial clock. We highlighted digital inconsistencies in the apparition: the pixel bleeding, duplicated star fields, unnatural motion blur. Seasoned coders joined in sharing threads breaking down the CGI anomalies.

Then Claire's voice rang out in the background of the stream, reading Matthew 24: *"If anyone says to you, 'Look, here is the Christ!' or 'There he is!' do not believe it..."*

Our stream ran barely two minutes—but it was enough. Underground channels lit up. The Remnant took the message and scattered it like seed.

Still, the deception worked.

Churches rang their bells in celebration, declaring the fulfillment of prophecy. They declared him the long-awaited *Messiah*. Not in metaphor, or symbol, the real one true god. A global interfaith council announced live from Jerusalem, the Vatican, Mecca, and New Delhi, the beginning of "spiritual unity." They spoke of a universal faith, one light for all the world. Some pastors wept on air, declaring "He's finally come." Crowds flooded the city squares, some bowing in reverence, others lifting their arms to the sky.

It didn't matter that scripture had warned of signs and wonders. It didn't matter that allegiance was demanded, not freely given. It didn't matter that the message sounded like light but felt...hollow. They believed and the whole world bowed.

But the Remnant stood. Scattered, quiet, but unwavering. Not against people, but against the lie.

Ezra shook his head as the broadcast flickered across the screen. "It's not the signs that matter. It's the source."

And we knew what the world didn't. Truth doesn't need a stage. It doesn't demand applause, dazzle, or manipulate. It endures, hidden in whispers, anchored in blood, and proven in the fire.

They followed the light because it glittered, but we followed the Word because it pierced.

When the world chose to bow...we remained standing.

Chapter Twenty-Five

Jalen returned under cover of night.

He looked thinner. Haunted. His skin windburned, eyes hollowed by the cold and the things he had yet to speak aloud. His shoulders carried silence like armor. But in his satchel, he held more than Margot's final notes. He came clutching a scroll.

Not a replica. Not an exhibit piece from a museum. An authentic, ancient scroll; sealed in wax and linen, preserved in a frozen monastery beneath the Antarctic ice shelf. It had been passed down by monks who had guarded its truth for generations.

Jalen didn't say much. But as I passed him a mug of coffee, he finally spoke, softly, eyes fixed on nothing. "The monastery had no heat. No sound. But it had prayers etched into the stone. Warnings. Names of stars erased from modern charts." He looked up, voice distant. "They knew. Long before us. They knew the sky was a clock... and someone's been trying to reset it."

Then he laid the scroll on the church table like a sacred fire. We didn't move, didn't breathe, even the lights seemed to dim as we gathered around.

Jalen's hands trembled as he unfolded the parchment. The ink was faded but the script was unmistakable: *"The heavens declare His handiwork; but a veil shall be stretched, and men shall forget the work of His hands. The veil shall remain until the time of remembering. In that time, the heavens shall tremble, and the false voice shall be broken by the shout of the Witnesses."*

It hit like thunder. Ezra spun around, grabbing his Bible and hurriedly flipping it open. "This matches Isaiah 25:7: *'He will destroy the shroud that enfolds all peoples, the sheet that covers all nations.'*"

I nodded. "And Daniel 12," I added, my voice barely audible. *"'Knowledge shall increase...and the sealed words shall be opened.'"*

The countdown, the alignments. This wasn't just astronomy, it was prophecy. The timing wasn't random, it had been appointed.

Then Jalen slid over the final page. A warning in Margot's hand: *"They will try once more. The final sign will eclipse all others. It will be beautiful. Believable. But not true. The only light you can trust is the one that never changes."*

Ezra stared at the page and then slowly looked up. "They're not just stars," he whispered. "They're lighthouses."

The world was searching for a savior.

But Heaven...Heaven was waiting for witnesses.

Chapter Twenty-Six

It came like thunder without a storm.

A single beam of light split the sky above Jerusalem. It wasn't weather. It wasn't a projection, at least not from any satellite anyone could trace. It appeared out of nowhere, descending in a slow, soundless column until it hovered above the Mount of Olives.

All over the world, the networks ignited. News anchors froze mid-sentence. Cameras shook. Crowds gathered in Times Square, in Nairobi, in São Paulo. Phones buzzed in millions of hands. Hashtags trended before most people even understood what they were seeing.

And then...the figure. Radiant. Human-shaped. Arms outstretched in a gesture that evoked every textbook image of holiness. Draped in robes. Glowing softly in the falling dusk. It hovered like a god descending.

"He's back," whispered broadcasters. "The one from the skies."

But something was off. This one didn't speak, didn't blink, didn't move. It didn't radiate anything, not peace, presence, nor love.

It just... *was*. Staged. Perfect. Hollow.

I stood before the monitor, Bible already open. "Matthew 24," I said calmly but tense.

Ezra flipped pages with urgency, his hands trembling just slightly. Then he read: *'Then if anyone says to you, "Look, here is the Christ!" or "There he is!" do not believe it. For false messiahs and false prophets will appear and perform great signs and wonders to deceive, if possible, even the elect...'*

I stepped forward, with my finger underlining the next verse. *"'For as lightning that comes from the east is visible even in the west, so will be the coming of the Son of Man.'"*

I then pointed at the screen. To the gleaming figure still suspended above the holy city. "That's not lightning," I whispered. "That's theater."

And in that moment, we knew what we had to do.

We needed to initiate the final broadcast. Not a test. Not a teaser. A full transmission, this was *our only chance to break through the veil of deception.*

The world was about to believe a lie.

I could feel it in the tone of the headlines, the eyes of the anchors, the way crowds gathered beneath screens like pilgrims at a shrine. The figure in the sky had spoken in seven languages. He quoted scripture out of order. He offered peace without truth.

And the world was ready to worship him.

Ezra checked the signal routing one last time. Jalen tightened the antenna clamps on the roof. The air buzzed with low-frequency tension. Our safehouse had become a control center: cables snaking across the floor, Scripture scrawled across walls, charts pinned to rafters.

The final broadcast would go live in 90 seconds. My palms were sweating. My heart raced like I was standing on the edge of something eternal.

Ezra handed me the mic. "You're the one they'll hear," he said.

"I'm not a prophet," I whispered.

"No," he said, smiling. "You're something scarier. You're clear."

I stepped into frame. The camera's red light blinked once. Then twice. Then held. And I began.

"My name is Claire Whitaker. I used to be a teacher. A skeptic. A woman of data, logic, and structure. And I still am. But today, I speak as a witness.

We've all seen it; the signs, the shimmer, the man in the sky. The promises. The unity. The light. But I need to tell you something, and you need to hear me clearly: Not all light is good, and not all signs are true. And most importantly not every savior is who he claims to be.

There's a verse—Matthew 24. It says: '*If anyone says to you, "Look, here is the Christ!" or "There he is!" do not believe it. For false messiahs will appear and perform great signs to deceive, if possible, even the elect.*'

That deception is not coming. It's here right now. You don't have to believe me. You probably won't. But I was one of you. I *am* one of you.

And I saw the veil. I saw the firmament tremble. I read the scroll they buried in ice. I watched the sky pulse like it remembered something we forgot.

Then I remembered, too.

I remembered the voice of a God I once left behind. A God who didn't demand my worship through fear or flash or force. But one who waited, whispered in a still small voice, and welcomed me home.

So, here's the truth, before the lie becomes law: The true Light doesn't shimmer. It doesn't glitch. It doesn't demand. It endures.

And when the sky breaks for real…you'll know Him by the sound of His voice. Not by the shine of His image."

The mic went quiet. I stepped out of frame, not to applause, but to a stillness deeper than silence. Jalen exhaled. Ezra nodded and then stepped into the frame.

"My name is Ezra Holt. I don't speak for a denomination. I don't speak for a party, a platform, or a movement. I speak as a man who watched the world stop looking up...and started worshiping everything beneath it. They told us the heavens were empty. That light was billions of years away and the rest was just math. But I've seen too much now. And what I've seen?

It's not silence. It's structure. A signal. It's a message waiting for someone with eyes to see. When the firmament trembled over that field, when the veil shimmered like breath caught between realms, I knew. Not everything we've called myth was meant to be forgotten. Some of it was hidden...until the time of remembering. This is that time. Scripture says in Isaiah 25: *'He will destroy the shroud that enfolds all peoples, the sheet that covers all nations.'*"

"That shroud is unraveling now. And what they offer you in its place, this glowing figure, this false peace, this manufactured savior, it isn't revelation. It's replication. They've tried to engineer the Second Coming. But you can't counterfeit the King and think the throne will stay empty. So, I'm sounding the alarm. As one of the witnesses, a watchman on the wall, a man who still believes the sky was made to declare the glory of God."

"And I'll say it clearly: The Messiah is not in your headlines. He will not descend through satellites. He will not speak from a podium. And He will not glitch. You'll know Him when He comes. You'll know Him by the scars. Until then, stay awake. Hold the line. And if the stars begin to sing... listen."

Ezra set the mic down gently. Claire nodded. No applause. No reaction. Just quiet. Truth doesn't always shout, sometimes it just waits to be recognized.

The signal was still live. For hours, feeds from hidden remnant strongholds began to light up the dark web. Encrypted frequencies spread from mountain cabins, underground chapels, refugee camps, and forest tents. They came from tribes with no country, believers with no platform, messengers with no names.

Scripture was read aloud in over twenty languages. Stellar charts were compared with ancient texts. The scroll was revealed—its prophecy laid bare. Hargrave's notes. Mason's frequencies. Margot's final warning. It was all poured out like oil on the altar.

The lie would go global in hours. But so would the truth. And finally, I wasn't just watching. I was witnessing.

And the people... listened.

Some with tears.
Some with fury.
Some with hands trembling over "share" buttons they never thought they'd press.

In university halls, students sat frozen.
In military barracks, soldiers turned their screens.
In cathedrals and cafes and cars and cellars... they watched. And they chose.

And then...the sky shimmered.

It was slight. Subtle. A flicker, like a curtain breathing in the wind. Above the Mount of Olives, the clouds wavered like a ripple passing through the air. The figure glitched.

Twice. Then once more. And just like that, it was gone. There was no thunder or lightning.
No second coming, just a vanishing. Like a program failing to load or a lie running out of power.

What remained was silence. Sacred. Seismic. Still. The three of us stared at the screen, not in awe... but in clarity. Not all who shine are Light and not all who perform signs are divine.

I closed my Bible and set it down gently. "The imitation was almost flawless," I whispered.
"But almost doesn't save."

Ezra nodded; his eyes filled not with triumph but resolve. "They're not just stars," he said again.

"They're lighthouses."

And now, the world had seen the difference. The false light had flickered. But the true Light still burned.

Chapter Twenty-Seven

We didn't expect applause. There was no celebration. No victory parade. Just a strange stillness, like the world was holding its breath. The broadcast had ended abruptly at 03:17 UTC.

We shut down the feed, dismantled the rigs, erased the routing trails. Some of the safehouses went dark immediately. Others stayed live, letting Scripture echo into the void for anyone still listening. The deception had failed, but the war wasn't over.

The response came twelve hours later.

Governments denied everything. The figure had been "an atmospheric illusion." The footage was "manipulated." And our broadcast? "Terrorist disinformation." Accounts were deleted, people arrested, others missing.

Ezra stood by the church window, arms folded, watching the night sky. "They didn't expect us to speak," he said. "And they sure didn't expect the world to listen."

I sat cross-legged on the floor, flipping through Hargrave's notes. "They'll try again," I said. "Maybe not tomorrow. But they will."

"They have to," Jalen added. "Because the real one's coming. And they're running out of time."

Outside, the wind moved through the trees like a warning. But above us...clear sky. Not broken. Not empty. Waiting.

Later that night, I went outside alone. The stars looked closer than they had before. Not because of some cosmic shift, but because I was finally looking with *open eyes*. I could see the design again. The order. The ancient clock still ticking. Somewhere beyond that veil, a King was watching. And somewhere beneath it, witnesses were waking up. They wouldn't be powerful nor famous, but ready.

I reached into my coat pocket and pulled out the last page of the scroll, the one Margot had translated in haste, in blood, in hope: "And they shall stand two by two, in cities and deserts, in ashes and gardens. And they shall not fear the fire, for they know the Light that does not change."

We weren't chosen because we were worthy. We were chosen because we were willing.

The firmament still held. But it wouldn't forever. When it finally cracked open, we'd be watching. Not with fear. But with truth and oil in our lamps.

Because when the sky opens for real...we will know the difference.

Epilogue

Margot:

She had stopped counting days. Somewhere above, the world had moved on, followed the light, the image, the lie. But down here, in the tunnels beneath the forbidden ice, truth still pulsed against stone walls. Silent. Alive.

They hadn't killed her. Not yet, as they still needed her to translate.

She smuggled one verse at a time onto scraps of cloth. Hid warnings inside code. Trusted someone would find them. Trusted Jalen, Ezra, and Claire were still out there. Trusted... even when she couldn't see the sky.

She pressed her hand to the wall of her cell. Beyond it, she could hear the humming; low, rhythmic. The sound of the machine coming back online. They were going to try again. But they still didn't know she still had one page they never found.

And the name on it...was Mason's.

Mason:

The light in the vault flickered, then stabilized.

He hadn't spoken aloud in weeks. Didn't need to. The machine responded to thought now. Or resonance. Or maybe faith. He hadn't decided which. The frequencies were aligning again. The stars were moving into place. The veil above was weakening, but so was the ground beneath.

They had looked up for signs, but they forgot to look down. He reached for the journal, now filled margin to margin. "The lie wasn't just in the sky," he wrote. "It was buried in our foundations."

Then he circled three letters he hadn't dared speak in months.

A. G. D.

And underneath them, one word: **Awakened.**

**Classified Transmission: Omega Protocol / Tier-7 Clearance
Source: Aeon Division—Orbital Relay Node 3**

"They know." The voice was calm, controlled. Not shaken, studying.

A figure stood before the screen in a black room. No windows. No clocks. Just layers of encrypted data scrolling past like scripture rewritten in code.

"The interference failed to suppress their feed. The signal breached containment in eight regions.
And now... faith is fracturing."

He paused. Zoomed in on an image frozen mid-transmission: Claire, standing before the parchment, the scroll opened. Truth in her hands.
"Witnesses have awakened. Which means Phase Two must advance."

Another voice crackled through the intercom, filtered and synthetic.
"Do they still believe they've won?"

A flicker of a smile. Not warmth—certainty. "Let them. The harder they hold their truth,
the deeper they'll dig. And that's where we'll find them."

He turned away from the screen and tapped a code into the console.

A hidden map appeared; one not of stars, but of foundations. Old cities.
Buried chambers.
Hollow ground.

"Initiate recovery teams. Deploy the shadow units. And reactivate Project Sheol."

He stared at the map, at a single blinking point deep in the Southern Hemisphere. "The veil may tremble...but the ground still holds secrets."

Continue the Journey... Coming Soon

The Veiled Truth Chronicles
Book Two: *The Weight of the Watchers*

The sky was never silent.
But the ground was never empty.

As the world turns its eyes to the light above, something older stirs below. Beneath ice shelves, ancient ruins tremble. Forgotten vaults groan beneath their seals. And the frequencies once mapped in stars now echo in stone.

Claire Whitaker thought she'd uncovered the deception. But it turns out, some truths were buried deeper than what one can see.

Bones once thought to be a myth are surfacing, names once whispered are returning, and something beneath the earth still remembers the Watchers.

The veil is thinning.
And the ground is breaking open.

Subscribe at jamarenbooks.com to be the first to read Chapter One.

Connect with JA Maren

@ja_maren_books

hello@jamarenbooks.com

jamarenbooks.com

facebook.com/jamarenbooks

About the Author

JA Maren writes across genres; from speculative fiction and prophetic mysteries to faith-based children's literature and Christian nonfiction.

Her stories blend biblical truth with imagination, asking deep questions and uncovering long-buried answers. In *The Veiled Truth Chronicles*, she explores a world where ancient prophecy collides with modern deception and where the heavens have not stopped speaking.

She is also the author of *The Paradox of Faith*, and the creator of the *Temperance Tilly* children's series, which is written for her daughter and inspired by the everyday adventures, bold questions, and hilarious honesty that only a child can bring.

When she's not writing, JA Maren is teaching, researching, raising a truth-loving girl, and looking up at the sky. Still watching and still listening.

Learn More at:
jamarenbooks.com

www.ingramcontent.com/pod-product-compliance
Lightning Source LLC
Chambersburg PA
CBHW030553130626
46552CB00006B/2528